4 KIDS in 5E & 1 CRaZy YeAR

Virginia Frances Schwartz

Holiday House / New York

For my nephew
Joe, on his graduation,
and
all my writing students
past, present,
and future

The extract on page 105 is reprinted with the permission of Simon & Schuster Books
for Young Readers, an imprint of Simon & Schuster Children's Publishing Division,
from *Fireflies!* by Julie Brinckloe. Copyright © 1985 Julie Brinckloe.

3   5   7   9   10   8   6   4   2

Library of Congress Cataloging-in-Publication Data

Schwartz, Virginia Frances.
4 kids in 5E & 1 crazy year / by Virginia Frances Schwartz.—1st ed.
p. cm.
Summary: Family, school, and life in general are seen through
the writings of four fifth graders who have been taken out of an overcrowded
New York City classroom and placed with a teacher who shows them
how to write and how to believe in themselves.
ISBN-13: 978-0-8234-1946-3 (hardcover)
ISBN-10: 0-8234-1946-0 (hardcover)
[1. Authorship—Fiction.   2. Schools—Fiction.   3. New York (N.Y.)—Fiction.]
I. Title.   II. Title: Four kids in fiveE and one crazy year.
PZ7.S4114Fou2006
[Fic]—dc22   2006041194
ISBN-13: 978-0-8234-2276-0 (pbk)

CONTENTS

REGISTER FOR 5E (22 kids):

BOYS (12)	GIRLS (10)
MAXIMO	DESTINY
GIOVANNI	ASHLEY
WILLIE	AMBER
MOHAMMED	CHELSEA
PETROS	DALMA
TAE HYUN	CARMEN
JACKSON	AH KUM
ANGEL	NATALIA
ASMIR	BO WAN
TYRONE	TIFFANY
RAMNEET	
LIN	

September

"Don't think too much.
Let your pencil do the talking."
–Ms. Hill

THE FIRST WORD

Destiny

I have seen the signs.

At 8 A.M. the sun hadn't hit our building yet like it did every single summer morning, teasing me to get up, get out, get playing. Far below our eighth-floor apartment, the street was still in shadow.

Marble notebooks are on sale in six-packs for $2.99.

If that's not enough hints for you, all-day barbecues smoke the air today: hot dogs, hamburgers, and beef patties, too.

1

You don't have to be a fortune-teller to figure it out.

It's Labor Day. School starts tomorrow.

Butterflies have landed in my belly and I won't eat a thing. I can't wait to see everybody. I have to tell them everything!

The phone keeps ringing for my mom. She's already been to three Parents' Association meetings at PS 1 in Queens, my school down the block. Fifth-grade parents are in an uproar. The gossip is thick as sea fog.

Nobody's happy. Not my principal, Mrs. Rosenblatt, who demands things her way. Not the teachers, who love things their way. Not the parents, who need things their way. This is the first time they all want the same thing—new classrooms! They complain that us fifth graders will be stuffed into sardine-tight rooms under a black tar roof on the tippy-top floor of PS 1. We'll have the biggest classes since 1920 when the building first opened to let in everybody's great-great-grandparents fresh off the boats that brought them to America. Psst . . . there's more . . . the city can't pay reading teachers so we don't have even one . . . all the

2

paraprofessionals who stop the little ones from crying got fired . . . and two aides are left to supervise lunch for 1,400 kids.

In the evenings, at those parents' meetings, parents yell a lot. My mom says families protest down at the district office, too. They holler so loud, you can hear them across the zooming parkway. Chelsea's mother can let go such a shrill scream, all the pigeons fly off. She's the president of the Parents' Association.

"Some kids are bigger than me!" she shouts over the phone today, waking up my dad snoozing in front of the television. "After Christmas, they'll be ten pounds heavier. How are so many kids going to fit in ONE room? We need another classroom for fifth grade RIGHT NOW!"

My mom frowns. "Wait, they told us in June. Families will move away. No-shows, they call kids who don't come back. But what about those parents registering new kids? The line was so long, it reached from the school to the subway entrance, four blocks away."

I have my own issues. On the last day of June, my best friend and I put our report cards side by side: 5A said Ah Kum's; 5D said mine.

We're gonna be living on two separate planets. Last year, Ah Kum and I were split apart in fourth grade. Looks like it'll be forever now.

Ah Kum's name suits her; in Chinese it means "orchid." She's a flower trying to bloom in a spot where it can't, like some shady garden, or poking out of a crack in the sidewalk.

"I'll be all alone without Ah Kum," I complained all summer.

"Maybe we won't be getting any more notes home about how much the two of you talk," my mom reminded me.

My dad said, "Maybe you'll learn more."

My sister, Lakeisha, just stuck her seven-year-old nose up in the air and grinned.

"See what happens." My grandma patted my braids. "Things have a way of working out. You and Ah Kum will find a way to be together."

The one and only bright spot about going back to school is a sneak peek at Willie. I can't even say his name without squealing. He'll be in 5C, down the hall. No, he did not tell me himself. I got it through the grapevine.

Willie only spoke to me once. Actually, he didn't really speak to me, but kind of said something so cool, I never forgot it. On Field Day, near the end of June, his soccer team won the tournament. Afterward, he smacked hands with a Jamaican buddy of his. It happened to be right by my ear.

Here's what he yelled: *"Everything cook and curry!"*

I don't know if they were talking about food (Cook? Curry? I am always hungry, too) or about the game. Whatever it meant, they high-fived it six feet up in the air. Willie's hair, a mess of dreadlocks, was flying, too. It sure is a stretch to understand how boys think. But now that I'm ten, it's the first task I'm gonna tackle in fifth grade: boy watching.

This brings me to the subject of clothes. Are you ready? Here's what PS 1 recommends for a successful start to fifth grade:

No midriffs
No tank tops
Nothing skimpy
Nothing sleeveless
Nothing too tight
Nothing above the knees

Excuse me, but what's left? A skirt, my grandma says. Not on me. Skirts stop at my thighs when they are supposed to halt at my knees. Even capris become shorts on me. Whatever am I going to wear? I can't show up with a cute little back-to-school outfit like Lakeisha. Her hair will be tied in pink ribbons and she'll wear a pleated jumper. I want to appear so cool like I just happened to be born in my clothes.

We went shopping on the avenue Saturday, past ten Korean nail salons, the bodega, the Jamaican meat pattie take-out window (hours 11 A.M. to midnight), the library with more closed hours than open ones, the city-bound subway entrance, Singh's Sweets, Peking Panda, where shrimp chow fun can be stir-fried in five minutes, and stopped at Old Navy.

I am now as ready as I can be. I got the clothes I wanted for the first day, a Jamaican meat pattie wrapped up for lunch, and the morning walk to school arranged with Ashley and her mom, and my friends Amber and Chelsea. But I'd gladly change back into my summer clothes, the jeans that got skintight and the T-shirt that is too skimpy, if I could be with Ah Kum.

Did I mention that I am not too crazy about my new teacher either? I have never met Mrs. Quinn personally. I did take a note to her once, but she never looked up from her desk. Just stuck her hand out to take it and went on working. She didn't take a second to have a peek at me. That tells me something. She's not interested in kids, just in teaching. I need a teacher who will like me as I am.

Here's what I want even though nobody asked. I wish we could put all the fifth graders in a giant extra-heavy tumbler like at Suds 'N Us Laundromat, then shake us and swirl us all around. Inside, we'd cling like magnets to our friends. Out we'd tumble, fresh and shiny new into each classroom with our friends smiling back at us like polished mirrors from across the aisles. For me, it's not about the number of kids. It's about Ah Kum and me. So either it's a jumble, a trip to Mrs. Rosenblatt's office to tell her this won't do, or else I'd be willing to try voodoo.

JELLY BEANS

Maximo

Mrs. McGonigle says Class 5B is like a peanut-butter-and-jelly sandwich squished flat. Forty kids squeeze into our classroom. Nearby, the other three fifth-grade classes have no desks left. I heard kids in 5C are standing because they don't have seats. On this September day in New York City, it's a scorcher—hot, hazy, and humid. Inside our rooms way up on the fourth floor, the temperature hits 94 degrees. It's like living in an attic.

Giovanni has a different way of putting it. He always does.

"*Ciao,* Maximo!" He whispers across the aisle. "You know those big jars of jelly beans you have to guess how many are inside?"

I shrug. I am deep into reading *Maniac Magee* and should have hung a DO NOT DISTURB! sign around my neck.

"That's us!" Giovanni grins. "We're all different shapes and sizes like those jelly beans. Different colors and flavors, too. Some are real smart like you. Quiet like Eunice. Funny like

Francesco. Artists like Jorge. We're all rolling around together like big beans."

I wish I could see the world through Giovanni's eyes. Everything would look sunshine bright. But I'm always lost in a mood. My moods are dull colors—drizzle gray or thunderstorm black. Giovanni can go along with anything. When he smiles, his freckles stretch, making me want to smile right back. Giovanni's tall with buckteeth and pointy black hair sticking straight up. There's a look of surprise on his face like he just hatched from an egg.

Giovanni's not bothered by the rumors Destiny's spreading around fifth grade. She's this in-your-face kind of girl from 5D. She'd better not get too close to my face, that's all I can say. Every day she broadcasts gossip about the parents protesting the big class sizes. What good does complaining do? We can see for ourselves. All the kids showed up this year when they said they would. Plus fifty new families. Even this morning, new kids are registering down in the office.

All we can hope is those new kids are not fifth graders. We are bulging here. When Tyler me ready to be given away with a flick of Mrs. McGonigle's hand.

They can't push me around like a checker piece anymore. I've been to three different schools already. I won't move again. I want to stay in one place.

I close my fist around the doorknob to go inside and let the teachers know, but Giovanni tugs my shirt. From down the hall, we both hear the click of high heels. The jingle of a hundred gold bracelets. Ten pointy artificial red nails are heading our way. It could only be Mrs. Rosenblatt, the principal. With a gasp, we lift off and bounce back the way we came, four flights down with barely a touch of our sneakers to the cement floor. Only the wind of our running is left behind with Giovanni's lunch. And the sickening slide of pink-and-blue cards building a new stack.

PLAYING CARDS

Giovanni

"Boys and girls!" Mrs. McGonigle announces. "Everyone sit up and listen. I have something very important to share with you."

I look up at the ceiling and suck air. I know what's coming. We're the kids nobody wants.

"Mrs. McGonigle will give us away," Maximo predicted. "Like leftovers in a garage sale."

I figured fifth grade was gonna go by and Mrs. McGonigle wouldn't ever know I have a problem. Since she hadn't spoken to my old reading teacher, Mrs. Rivera, I thought I was safe. Mrs. Rivera was gone, gone, gone. She lost her job because the mayor wouldn't pay her. That's what this girl Destiny said. So my own teacher hadn't guessed I couldn't read yet. Mrs. Rivera didn't show up at the door anymore like something was missing from me that I could get from her. She thought I could just leave for a while and get smart with her. But it never happened.

It isn't that I can't read exactly. Most of the words, except the big ones, I can sound out. I just don't see what the fuss is about. String all those words together in a novel, the kind of book we are supposed to be reading in fifth grade, and there's too much happening. That's how it is in my house, too. If my teenage brother, Mario, is home, the stereo is blasting on? When Mrs. McGonigle finds out I can't read, she won't take it all that well. She's the oldest teacher in the building, with white streaks in her hair that Amber says are natural. She guesses every trick we try before we even think it. Maybe I can volunteer to go.

"Chelsea!"

Heads go down. Eunice winces, pressing her hand over her belly. She eyes the door like she needs to bolt to the bathroom. Jorge does not doodle for the first time ever. His pencil is frozen in his hand.

"Mohammed!"

He sits straight up like linguini ready to pop into a pot. He's usually sprawled on his desk, snoring.

One more blue card left. Mrs. McGonigle announces the last name.

"Giovanni!"

Salute! I'm in the trade! Across the room, Max's head jerks my way. A tiny smile creeps over his lips. But the other kids in 5B stare at us like we have boogers sticking out of our ears. The six of us will step into a kind of place no fifth grader ever went before. It's like we are leaving for planet Pluto.

"Who's gonna go with us from the other classes?" Amber whispers.

Whoever it is, I hope they can't read.

LOST IN A DAYDREAM

Willie

I'm in a September daze. You know the kind where you cannot believe your mom is yelling at such an hour. She's shaking my shoulders and won't stop. I know my room is *chaka-chaka,* with wide-open suitcases full of dirty clothes spilling out. But, it's not that.

"WILLIE! *MOVE YOUR BACKSIDE NOW!* You'll be late for SCHOOL!"

On the way to PS 1, I see the other kids spreading over the blocks, slow and quiet, like ants marching in a long line. They've all got gel and spiky haircuts and new jeans. School begins this year at 8:20 A.M., and it's a shock I'm never gonna recover from.

All I can think of is summer mornings at my grandma's house in Jamaica.

. . . When your feet hit the floor all by themselves. Nobody calls you. No one's even looking for you.

the right word for everything. When she says something, it always sounds funny.

Then I see the new teacher, Ms. Hill, roaming the aisles, pointing to our seats—four groups of double rows, with the desks facing one another. She's tall, skinny, and fussing like my mom cooking Sunday dinner. Only she's not serving curry goat with roti. She's dealing in kids. She doesn't seem at all like Mrs. Nelson, who sat at her desk peering at us like a cat over the top of her reading glasses. Her eyes caught every movement. No mouse would have a chance with her. We held our breath when we lined up at her desk for homework check. She had stale coffee breath all day long.

Ms. Hill points to my desk at the very end of one row. That's where I always go since I'm tall. It faces the big windows that line one whole wall of the classroom. I don't set my books down. Just stare out the window at the silent back street where an old maple tree rises above the apartment buildings. There's a little drop of yellow in its leaves. This is a seat for a daydreamer. It won't feel like I'm locked inside, with summer gone.

Then I check out the other kids. Giovanni

finally sits down. He waited in the doorway, his eyes big and round, but he wouldn't step inside. He looked like he was studying the ceiling instead. Last year Gio and I played soccer in the yard after school. If you could call it that. He'd rather juggle than play, keep the ball floating in the air as long as he can, without ever touching down. By the time Ms. Hill notices Gio, there's only one seat left at the back, across from Max.

I remember Max from second grade in Miss Chu's class. We were friends right away. But then something happened. I heard his mom split from his dad. They all disappeared overnight. Max's forgotten book bag hung in the closet like a ghost. When he moved back last spring, he acted like he didn't remember me. Maximo was closed up tighter than a conch in its shell. He sat in the room, but he was elsewhere.

"Welcome to 5E!" Ms. Hill's soft voice cuts into my thoughts. "You were chosen to come into this room. Do you know why?"

All eyes land on her. It's so quiet I can hear Mohammed swallow.

"Because 5E stands for excellence," she

"Now it's time to write. Jot the date on top of your page and begin. Make a list of ten noticings."

"Only in this room?" Jackson calls out.

"Anywhere! Now—no more questions!" Ms. Hill shoots back. "Don't think too much. Let your pencil do the talking."

She shuts the lights off and sits right down in the empty desk across from me. We sneak peeks at her. With a firm hand, she presses a pencil to her notebook page, scratching away like a hen pecking dirt. She does not lift her head. We have no choice but to do the same. She's ignoring us.

My thoughts buzz around in my head like mosquitoes. Wish I could swat them flat. I'm circling around and around something I really want to say.

There is this place calling me. A faraway place. A long plane trip away and then a forever ride in a bouncing bus along the left side of the road, leaning into the curves of the hills until it's dark and you're there. Down a dirt lane beneath the pinpoint dots of a million stars. The damp smell of the sea, stretching out where you can't see it, endless in the night.

When Ms. Hill flicks the lights back on later, I blink. On the desk in front of me, my notebook is blank. All around me, hands reach for the air, begging to share their work—Ashley, Jackson, Natalia, Bo Wan. Who will she pick?

It better not be me.

SITTING UP HIGH

Destiny

You can spot me in Ms. Hill's class easy. I'm the one with my mouth wide open, chatting and grinning. My head sticks up like a groundhog in spring. The groundhog is big time. He gets to make major decisions about the weather. All the world watches him. He just looks around with those perky eyes. *Snap!* He's got the scoop. Everyone hangs on what we say.

Being tall is a blessing, my mom says. You get to see the world from a different place. You see what others don't because you're looking down at the top of their heads. Most people see just what's in front of them. Not me. I get the whole landscape. I'm a people person. I sit in the center of the class and see everything. Yes, I said everything. My eyes scan the room like a security guard, not that sleepy guy we got sitting by the front door of PS 1 but a real live one. I'm going into public relations and communication. Know what I wanna do? Represent rap stars. Make up their schedules. Arrange interviews and trips. Organize them. They're dreamers. They need me.

I could just squeeze myself. This is my dream class! Let me chant the names: Chelsea! Amber! Ashley! Willie!!! The beat goes on. Here's the biggest scoop of all! Ah Kum and I are together again. And I didn't need voodoo either.

Ah Kum is just three seats away. Her eyes open like petals when she turns my way. She's dainty, all three and a half feet of her. She's the size of my sister Lakeisha in second grade, the one who used to follow me around like I was the sun and she was the day. Now my sister's Miss Smarty Pants and getting a fresh mouth besides. Being with Ah Kum reminds me of the way it used to be. Someone always looking up to me, and me leaning my elbow on her shoulder. Someone by my side, laughing at all my jokes. That girl needs light and laughs and I'm the one to do it.

Ms. Hill's the one I have to thank for being here. She must have picked me. Most of the other teachers kept Ah Kum and me at opposite ends of the building. So I'm gonna do all I can to please her. I pledge my allegiance to Ms. Hill. I promise not to call out, distract anyone, or pass notes. I will always listen to the lesson. Okay?

Ms. Hill wants noticings. I'm into that. She needs a date on top of the page? No problem. I'm gonna scratch away just like I see her doing. Except I don't have a gauzy skirt that looks like a spider spun it when my teacher fans it out to sit down. So I'll squeeze into my seat with my sequined T-shirt that shines in the sunlight and beams these words: *Hard Rock Café*. Did I mention my wide-bottomed jeans with slits that open and are decorated in red plastic jewels? It's my back-to-school outfit that I wear most days.

Time to let my no. 2 pencil loose.

9/27 OBSERVATIONS (Boy Watching)

I'll start with Gio. He's nice all the way through. Plus he's got a thick head of hair. That hair is wild with a mind of its own, pointing every which way. A girl gets an urge to comb it. His eyes are like the deep black holes of outer space. You could get lost in them. You wouldn't believe his eyelashes. There's like a million of them, curly and fanned out around those eyes.

Mohammed is nearby. He's filled out with muscles. He sits like an empty drum most of the time. When it's time to work, he moves in slow motion. He hates math, writing, and most subjects, except gym.

Tyrone's drifting like a fly. Always frowning. Never happy until the final bell rings.

Willie's quiet. Lean as a drumstick. Watch the quiet ones, my grandma says, but I don't know why. Jamaica's written all over that hair. His dreadlocks must weigh fifty pounds, more than the rest of him. They twirl. They twist. They knot. They mat. Cool! He doesn't have to comb them—ever! The only thing, though, is he never looks my way.

Now it's Max's turn. You know how some people just get under your skin? You take one look at them and feel itchy like you need to scratch. That's what Max does to me. He's restless as a lion in a cage, drumming his claws on the desk, waiting to pounce. Books calm him down. Max and novels are bound together like glue. He'd rather read than have a conversation. Now what kind of person is that?

"Psst!" I bug Chelsea. "Where did *he* come from?"

"Who, Max? I was in kindergarten with him. He spent every afternoon in time-out. He never got to play. He moved away, but he came back last spring. He doesn't talk to girls. Guess where his mom works?"

I shrug.

The scent of sour grapes comes from her mouth. Bet it's candy.

"The Steinway Nursing Home."

Hmm . . . I sit up, my back groundhog straight. There's a story there. It's worth investigating. And I know how. Take a look at my star-studded wardrobe and you know I have connections. My mom's the secretary at the Steinway Nursing Home. That place is famous. Everyone in the borough knows it's where Vinny the Hammer's grandmother lives. Vinny's the heavyweight contender people in Queens bet on in the boxing ring. They say he's a real hunk. My mom saw the back of him once. Bleached blond hair. Shoulders like a football player. His whole family visits the nursing home. Vinny's grandmother watches all his boxing matches on cable TV. Whenever he's got a hold on somebody, she cheers "HOOK 'EM, VINNY!" so loud, the other old folks yank their hearing aids out.

My mom sees everything there, believe me. Secretaries look like they're sitting still minding their paperwork, but, believe me, they've got ears. Everyone confesses secrets to them. I'm going to get the whole scoop on Max and nothing but the scoop. Just wait!

OCTOBER

"But where should I
begin my story?"
–Giovanni

WE'RE IN BUT I'M OUT

Maximo

It's no surprise when Ms. Hill assigns me a
seat at the back of the room. Teachers take one
look at me and make up their mind I'm
trouble. Maybe it's the hair, all four inches of it
standing straight up, shiny and wet with gel.
The stud earring. Or the way I slide down in
my seat like I have no backbone at all.

Then there's my hands. They have a mind
of their own. Tap, tap, tapping a pencil on my
desk. Shooting eraser shavings across the aisle.
Sometimes I wake up in the middle of the

31

night and my hands are balled up in fists. They've been that way a long time. I don't want to remember what it was like way back when, but sometimes scenes play out in my mind. They run like a movie. Once it starts, I have to watch.

There's one scene that keeps coming back. It happened loads of times. I don't remember all of it, but my mom says it began when I was born. Something changed my dad. My mom didn't have to say that it was me.

Me, stepping into the shadows. Sharp yells. Then the stinging sound. Big hands smacking bare flesh. My mother fell down. I wanted to help her, pummel my fists into my dad's back. But I was too small. I was invisible watching from the shadows with my fists jammed in my pockets. I don't know who I was more angry at—my dad for hitting my mom, or myself for not moving one inch to stop him.

My mom says my dad couldn't handle raising a kid. He was still a kid himself. He wasn't prepared. I am the kid nobody wants. Not Mrs. McGonigle. Or Mrs. Rosenblatt. Surely not Ms. Hill. Why would they want me if my own dad didn't?

I blow out a sigh to break the spell I'm in and look around 5E. Another place I never chose. Another class I don't want to be in. Too many girls for one thing. Then there's that busybody Destiny who wormed her way into 5E. I heard she practiced voodoo so she could switch classes. She's always eyeballing me, sneaking a look my way. But why did Mrs. Rosenblatt stick me in this class? She knows I hate writing. That's all we do in this class. I always get "Unsatisfactory" in writing on my report cards. Our principal reads every report card. I ought to know because she always compliments me for 4 in reading. That's the top mark.

Ms. Hill calls us to the Writers' Circle, which is a pile of kids sitting on an ugly purple rug around the teacher's feet. What would I wanna do that for? Ashley sure wants to do it for she is first, up so close that Ms. Hill's long dress drapes in front of her. Chelsea slides next to her. Destiny leans on Ah Kum like she's a lamppost. Petros and Ramneet slide into place like they are hitting home plate. Everyone rushes to sit beside a friend and a chance to go somewhere. I am the last one to join in.

Giovanni saves a place for me, patting it with his hand to keep it available.

"Here's your parking space." He grins.

When I finally sink to the floor, I don't cross my legs into a pretzel like Ms. Hill asks, but push them straight out. It's the first time I see the new teacher up close. She wears lavender lipstick with nail polish to match. Or maybe it's violet. She must be happy to wear such a bright color. My mom never would. She mostly wears a white pantsuit, her uniform at the Steinway Nursing Home. She's a nurse's aide, which means she does all the hard work on the day shift without the big paycheck the head nurse gets. Evenings, she sticks to black clothes. My mom shops in Old Navy right along with me, and she looks crumpled at the end of the day. Not Ms. Hill. She wears a long flower power dress that moves when she does. She kind of flows like water. Her brown curls are highlighted with blonde streaks. The girls lean forward, as if they are going to hear secrets.

"Today we are going to write about place. I'll tell you about a place I love."

Silence. You can see a wondering light up everyone's eyes as kids study our new teacher.

Bet she's gonna be another one who won't let us breathe.

"I grew up on a farm in Canada. My grand-father planted an orchard of trees just before I was born. They grew in long, straight lines like soldiers. Apples. Cherries. Peaches. In May the smell of their blossoms was like perfume. I knew every tree. That's where you'd find me, hanging upside down or lying across a branch, reading a book."

She waits. It's our turn now.

"I been to Canada!" Jackson blurts out. "Niagara Falls."

"Tell us about it," Ms. Hill says.

"There's this awesome waterfall gushing down. We sailed so close to it in a boat that we got soaked. It felt cool on such a hot day."

Ms. Hill points her thumb straight up. "Great details, Jackson! You always seem to start 5E talking."

I think about my apartment and wonder if I could write about that. It's not a place I'd call home. A one-room studio with a curtain hanging between my mom's bed and mine. We've lived there six months and haven't unpacked all the boxes yet. My mom is too busy. Sometimes she works double shifts to earn overtime. She starts work by 7 A.M. and comes back at midnight. That's when you see the white of the bare fridge. Dinner those days is peanut-butter sandwiches. I look forward to school lunch.

All around me the other kids brag about places they visited. Not me. Hey, if I get to the diner on the boulevard this weekend, I'll die happy.

Ashley describes Disneyland while everyone sighs. Her eyelashes are so blonde, they look like they are spun from gold. A long coil of coppery hair dangles in her face. I remember how in second grade I thought she was a princess straight out of a fairy tale.

Next to me, Giovanni rolls his big, dark eyes. Teachers think he doesn't pay attention. But he can stare at Ashley a full twenty minutes without blinking. That's real concentration. He's trained his eraser to do forward flips and back bends like it's in the Olympics. He looks at everything, even a speck of dust, with amazement.

He raises his hand. "What about upstate?"

Ms. Hill nods as Giovanni continues. "I go

there sometimes. There's big mountains and it's so cold. Once we saw some deer in the woods. They were running away. But first, they just stood still and looked at us."

"That will make a great story, Giovanni," Ms. Hill tells him.

Giovanni blurts things out without thinking. He mostly mutters *"Scuzi!"* He twists his lips now, puzzled that the teacher liked what he said. Ashley examines him like she never saw him before. Her plump lips hang open.

Next Ms. Hill shows us pictures of the prairie. We'll be studying it in social studies. I already know about it. You could never forget what the prairie looks like if you read *Sarah, Plain and Tall*. All around me, kids shoot out describing words. The teacher writes a list on the blackboard:

flat and dry
long, hot summers
cold in winter
tall grasses
farms
quiet

Then she reads a picture book by the same author, called *What You Know First*. She said the author grew up on the prairie but left it behind forever when she was young. She loved it so much, though, that she always writes about it. The pictures are black-and-white sketches that look frozen in time, like old photographs. There are just a few words to each page. The words have a sadness behind them, a slowness, as if it hurts to look back. I stare at the tree on the cover. The author tells about the cottonwood tree that grew on the prairie, a tree she says good-bye to. She will never see it again.

There was a pine tree behind the old building we lived in when I was in second grade at PS 1. That tree was tall and pointy. It marked home plate where my dad taught me baseball. Then all at once, a memory leaks out.

I remember the loud fight awakening me and the door slamming. I peeked out the window and saw my dad walking away beneath that tree. I turned my head only a few seconds because I heard my mother dragging our back-packs out and filling them with all our stuff.

"We have to leave now," she panted, between quick breaths. "We have to go someplace safe." The bruises were deep purple beneath her eye. When I looked back outside, he was gone. Just the tree stood there. I never saw my dad again.

The light monitor shuts the lights off. Ms. Hill stands up and everyone goes back to his or her desk to write. I am the last one to leave. When I pass by Giovanni's desk, he doesn't look up. His pencil pumps across the notebook page as if it's in a race. Across the room Willie stares out the window at the maple tree. I wonder if he notices how, overnight, fire red has splashed the yellowing leaves. Soon those leaves will fall. Overnight your life can change. You just wake up the next day and it's like that. Nothing you can do to stop it.

All these kids talk about their lives. How can I tell anybody I lived in a shelter for abused women, under a court order of protection? Even when they sent me for counseling at the shelter, I zipped my lips real tight. I never said a word about how I hated my dad. Yet I missed him back then, too.

Not one word drops onto my page now.

DEAR OH DEER

Giovanni

When I hear that book, I get shivers. The prairie is such a still, flat place. The author got it all down just right as if she took a snapshot and captured it. *Click!* Her words go.

I see pictures, too. My mind snaps photographs just like in the book. Patches of black earth sticking out of the snow. The brown doe with her spotted fawn nearby. How she stared at us like a statue. When my brother, Mario, spoke, it broke the spell. The deer shot away. Her legs bounced high and her tail flew.

But where should I begin my story? The trip there? How we had to rush to get ready, eleven people crammed into my uncle's minivan, my aunt yelling because my sister ran back to get her curling iron, Mario shoving me the whole way. By the time we got there, it was so black, you could see stars from the top of the sky all the way down to the edge of the land.

My new teacher wants pictures with words. She doesn't want the trip part. "Get right into the action," she said. "Focus on the best part of your story." My head drops down to track the words on the page. Then I pause to think about how to spell "bonced."

I look around. The only ones not working are Tyrone and Willie. Tyrone still hasn't bought a writer's notebook. Willie's staring out the window. Max says Willie's cool. He's the only kid we know who can do a bicycle kick. He sure can play soccer, but can he spell?

I'll bug Maximo. He's closer. "*Scuzi!* How do you spell bonced?"

He's in some kind of trance. But he writes the word on the notebook I shove on his desk: *bounced.* Then he doodles all over his page.

I have the word. I'm zooming! I get so much stuff down and then draw a picture to go with it that I don't see her at first. Ms. Hill stands right beside my desk. Her long hair shines with blonde highlights that Amber says cost a lot of money. Amber certainly corrected Maximo about the name of the teacher's nail polish. It's Candy Baby, she swears. Amber should know. She lives above a Korean nail salon. Max didn't like that one bit. He wants to be the one who knows everything.

Gulp! I am in big trouble. Ms. Hill reads

spilled into the air here like a permanent school file. I am going to turn out just like my brother. In a flash I see my old report card: "Below Standard in Reading."

Ms. Hill must have heard those words, too. The very next week the hold-over letter arrives in the mail. It was signed by both her and the principal. That's official. My mom shook her head quietly and promised not to show it to my dad. Every grade it comes, a dark warning, brewing over my head like a boiling pot of espresso the whole year long.

10/25

i think about the poor deer. how she stood still on that hill, hoping she was invisible. if we were hunters with a gun, she'd be the purrfect target.

i look around the classroom and count all the students up and down the rows. Why didn't i notise it before? There's twenty-one, including me. Not 40 like in 5B.

we are not like jelly beans in a jar anymore. we can be seen.

It won't be any different with Ms. Hill. My new teacher is on to me. I am not an excellent student. I tried as hard as I could. The hold-over letter came anyway. Words were popping out of me like popcorn. That never happened in my writing before. Didn't she notice?

But it still isn't good enough. I can tell. I can always tell.

WRITERS' WALK

Willie

Words pound like drumbeats in my head. *"Night is so quiet in the country. Light to dusk. Dusk to dark."* I swirl with the leaves falling down in the playground after lunch. Giovanni spreads his arms and swoops at me like a big crow. *"Then the night creatures awaken: frogs, rabbits, and owls."* I wave my arms like big wide wings and caw at Gio. I am flying right inside Cynthia Rylant's book *Night in the Country,* in and out of the words to another place. Max caws back, leaning against the fence, watching us.

Today we go on the Writers' Walk. The permission slips are handed in, and Giovanni's aunt and mom wait by the front steps of the school, ready to go with us. They look puzzled about what we are doing.

"*Che cosa?* You are going on a walk to the park to find your senses?" Gio's aunt stands on the other side of the playground fence.

Giovanni had not explained it right. Max steps up to the fence.

"We are going to write about everything we notice using our senses," he says. "We have five—seeing, hearing, smelling, tasting, and touching."

Giovanni's aunt stops chattering and stares at us. His mom squeezes her purse tightly. She wears short capri pants with bare legs and spiky heels. I sure hope she can walk all the blocks to the park in them.

Hey, *mon,* there's another sense, I want to tell Max. It's inside, how something makes you feel. But I don't say a word to Max. Besides, he and Gio are tight. Giovanni might join in my games awhile, but he always runs back to Maximo's side. The two of them fit like puzzle pieces. I wonder why. They are so different. Maybe one's got what the other's missing.

Then Ms. Hill appears. Sneakers poke out beneath her long skirt. She brings her note-book and pencil and so do we. But we also carry soccer balls and jump ropes. She reminds us about keeping the writer's rules, stopping to write what we observe as we walk.

"What will you do with your pencils?" she calls out to us.

Angel wiggles his body like a worm. "Keep them moving."

"What about your voices?" she asks.

"Silence until after we share in the park!" Tae Hyun shouts the answer like an order.

We all laugh and salute him. We step onto the sidewalk behind the tall brick school where everyone is closed up inside. The sidewalks are wet from last night's rain. Gray clouds hang above our heads. We stop beneath the maple tree. Hundreds of leaves cling to the sidewalk. Polka-dotted red leaves. Rusty leaves. Our pencils scratch away. Mohammed and Tyrone sketch, and I do the same. Lin does not know what to do. He can't read or write or say one word in English. He just moved here from China last week.

We move on. A grinning pumpkin sits on a windowsill. On top of a fence, a plastic skeleton shivers in the wind. A flock of crows startles us, cawing overhead. There's so much to see when you're looking.

Stepping off the curb, new words begin to beat in my head:

Gray skies. End of things. All the birds fly away. . . . My grandma waving from the porch. Her arm moving slowly as if it hurt to push the air. Her salt-and-pepper hair tied up in tight braids on top of her head. How she leaned on the pillar, her eyes following our bus . . .

Then, *poof,* I'm out of the daydream. The pictures in my head disappear quick as meat patties from a plate. I should have written them down. They were like no words I knew.

Up and down the sidewalk around me, all the notebook pages are filling except mine and Max's. Maximo stares at clouds drifting by. Giovanni presses his notebook flat against Max's back and writes. Jackson flips a page. Ms. Hill jots down notes in quick script. A wind kicks up. I huddle inside my jacket.

Words stick in my throat. They want to creep out, but I won't let them. I tighten my lips, pushing them back down. Wish *everything was cook and curry,* but it's not. Suddenly little wheezes whirl in my chest, and there's this feeling that I can't breathe. I pop the inhaler into my mouth just in time. This damp air brings my asthma on.

At the park we want to run and swirl with the leaves, but Ms. Hill gathers us together in a circle first to share our noticings.

"It's misty." She looks around. "I was worried it would rain."

Ashley reads: "The sky hangs down, so gray. I could hardly see the trees in the park. They looked like ghosts, far away."

That one puts the shivers through me.

"It's hushed outside," reads Chelsea. "No one is out but us. It's like everything is waiting because fall is here."

Suddenly a brand-new poem pops out of Destiny. Her pencil just lifted off the page this moment. She's such a *chatabax,* she can't keep it to herself one second. She shouts it out to everyone in the whole park, like some street vendor selling mangoes. Even the moms pushing baby carriages in the distance stop to listen.

October Sights
Did you see that skeleton swinging
in the wind

like he had no backbone at all?
He was grinning.
That's when the crows
flew by
cawing out—
it's Halloween!

Everyone claps and shouts. Destiny twirls high in the air. Her whole face shines like she has sunlight trapped inside. All around her, on this gray day, the girls spin, leaping up, to be as tall as her. Ah Kum lifts up, too, tiny as a dust ball, beside Destiny's daddy-long-spider legs. My grandma would laugh and call Destiny a *labba-mout,* yet that girl caught in words how we all feel and just let it loose. Wish I could do that.

Ms. Hill dismisses us with a wave. The boys spread out across the park. Onto the grass we race to blast the soccer ball sky-high and shout.

But when my feet land a half hour later, I wonder again—

How did those words come to me?

Will they come again another time?

GOSSIP COLUMNIST

Destiny

I'm bustin' here. I got the scoop from my mom about Max's mom, Maria: why she came back to this neighborhood, what happened to them before, and what she secretly plans on doing. Bet Max doesn't even know about it yet. There's a rumor circling around the Steinway Nursing Home, too. You would think it's a boring place with a lot of sleepy old people, but it's not. I can't tell you about it, though. My mom told me not to. But Chelsea keeps bugging me to spill it. And if I don't let Ashley in on it, she won't tell me what she thinks about Giovanni. I see her sneaking peeks at him. So, I jot down some of the juicy parts and slip notes both ways down the aisles to Chelsea and Ashley.

Don't ever underestimate a beautiful teacher, one that looks like a fairy godmother, even if she does act like a poet. In a flash she snaps up those notes like they were string beans. My head drops way down to the desk, but my eyes watch her. She reads the notes! She doesn't say a word, though. Math comes and goes and then reading. All the while the clock strikes a beat, "You're in troub-le! You're in troub-le!"

Max smirks the whole time. His eyes shift back and forth from me to Ms. Hill. His shoulders shake from trying not to laugh out loud. He elbows Petros next to him. Petros laughs at anything. Give him a breeze, and it'll tickle him into giggles. Max is getting even with me for bugging him at lunch. But I was just trying to figure out what he knew.

"Hey, Max, do you ever go shopping on the boulevard?" I asked him.

He shrugged. "Sure. Plenty."

"Well, my mom and I were shopping for clothes and guess who we ran into? Your mom. She was in Candees."

"My mom does not go to Candees. She shops in Old Navy."

"Well, she not only went in there, but she bought something, too. It sure will look nice on her."

Max had frowned and turned away. But he had answered my question. He doesn't know what's going on with his own mom.

Finally Ms. Hill calls me up to her desk.

I'm at her elbow, flashing my trademark grin.

"Yeah . . . yes, Ms. Hill," I stutter. "I'll do anything for you. Whip that file down to the office. Clean your desk. I'd even braid your hair in a million tiny blonde strands if you wanted it."

Then I catch the look in her eyes. It's stern as a STOP sign.

"Destiny, you need to think before you tell other people's business. Perhaps they will mind. Did you ever think of that?"

"No, Ms. Hill, I mean, I promise not to do it again."

"Good. I won't write down what happened today. But, if it should ever happen again, I will. I don't want to worry your family. Or make them aware that instead of doing your work, you are passing notes."

I do not speak for the rest of the day. I do not even look at Max. I know he is gloating.

Most everyone is stepping lightly because of the Halloween Parade. Nobody wants to get grounded and miss it. It's a magical day when we get to be somebody besides ourselves. This year we have to be storybook characters. Literary people, says Ms. Hill. I know exactly what to be. I'm the girl writer, the one who spies on everybody in *How to Get Famous in Brooklyn.* I wear blue-jean overalls and carry my writer's notebook in one hand, a magnifying glass in the other, and a pencil behind my ear.

On Halloween, we march around the school block with all the parents and neighbors cheering and pointing at our costumes. Even the retired folks poke out of their buildings, set up lawn chairs, and gawk at us. The principal leads the parade in a black tuxedo with a starched white shirt. She waddles. Hey! She's the penguin from *Mr. Popper's Penguins.* Behind her is the assistant principal, Pippi Longstocking, in red-and-white-striped kneesocks. Max wears floppy sneakers, sweatpants, and holds a book in one hand. I thought he was himself, but Chelsea says no, he's Maniac Magee. Willie's an old man in a baggy suit and spectacles carrying a birdcage, like the grandfather from *Grandfather's Journey.* Gio walks on all fours with uncombed hair and raggedy clothes. He's the dog from *Because of Winn-Dixie.* One thing's for sure. I'm going to have to get caught up on my reading.

We don't recognize Ms. Hill at first. She

wears a long skirt to her ankles, a frilly blouse, silk jacket, reading glasses on her nose, a wide-brimmed hat, and dried flowers everywhere—on her hat, pinned to her jacket, and in her hands, a big bouquet.

"They're lupines," she says. "Miss Rumphius planted them all around her cottage by the sea. She wanted to make the world more beautiful. And she did. It was something she promised her grandfather before he died."

After the parade, spread out on the rug, we all study the book, *Miss Rumphius,* that our teacher holds up. The main character looks as elegant as Ms. Hill. She has flowers to plant; Ms. Hill has kids to teach. We all have talents. Mine's in the way I look at people. When I saw the penguin and the dog in the parade, it got me thinking about animals.

10/31

I'm in to animals. So is Cynthia Rylant. She was brought up on a farm with loads of animals like snakes, chickens, and cats. If you look carefully through her books, you will always spot pets. Take *The Relatives Came.* There's even a dog lying upside down at the family sleepover. Ms. Rylant says animals bring out the truth in people. Well, I say people remind me of animals.

Ms. Hill's a swan. Elegant. She glides around the room like she's sailing over water. She always looks like she knows exactly where she's going.

Gio is like the deer he writes about. He doesn't have a mean bone in his body. He's gentle. Those saucer eyes of his look innocent and startled like a deer caught in the headlights. There's something untamed about him.

Willie's a lion cub with those dreadlocks. He has no idea how cuddly he looks. He sits still, his hazel eyes daydreaming, in a jungle of his own. He lends me pencils when I ask, even if it's every day (which it is). He speaks to me in Jamaican like I understand. "Here, sistren," he says, handing me a pencil. It makes me feel like I'm part of his family.

Now that Max. He's got a chip on his shoulder, and he's always mad. All I asked was where he moved from. He nearly bit my head off like a pit bull, all growly. He'd better stop his scowling or that look will stick on his face and he'll turn into one ugly old man. At least, that's what my grandma always says.

Change is sure going to come to that boy, don't I know it.

NOVEMBER

"Writing makes you drift
and dream and say things
you don't even plan on."
–Destiny

THE EDGE

Maximo

The day is November gray. Cloudy. All the light feels sucked out of the sky. This morning my mom called me "edgy." I was sulking at breakfast. I begged her to get me out of Ms. Hill's class. I'd even go back to Mrs. McGonigle's, I bargained with her. I didn't tell her I had already spoken to Mrs. Rosenblatt about it. It never went further than a cold stare.

"I know you're disappointed about how things turned out in our family," my mom said. "But I am doing my best to make it right now.

Don't make being in 5E another problem. It's an opportunity."

Right about then I woke up, and all I did was smell the coffee brewing in our galley kitchen. My mom was going to a workshop today. Instead of her uniform, she wore a sky blue paisley skirt that swished when she sat down next to me. Her top was pastel blue. It magnified her light blue eyes. This was not an Old Navy outfit. I hate to admit it, but Destiny was right. It had the kind of soft colors I'd seen in the windows of Candees. Cheap stuff, strictly for girls. My mom was not a girl. Something was up. My eyes ate her up, instead of my breakfast.

"Since we left your dad, I've been a mess. But"—my mom took a deep breath—"I want to put it behind us. I don't want to be angry or sad anymore. I want to let it go. Start again. That's what I want you to do, too."

"How can I? Dad just disappeared. We ran off."

"Max, your dad won't be coming back to us." Her lips flattened. "He owes too much money. He gambled, bought expensive cars we couldn't afford. Piled it on the credit cards. I've been paying all his bills. I'll be paying them my whole life. So, I'm considering something. But I wanted to talk to you first."

A long pause. I could feel my heart revving up, faster and faster, taking off without me.

"I want to track your father down. An agency will do it for free. If they find him, they'll make him pay his own bills and child support, too. It's the law. We could rent a bigger apartment. Get you a bike. Maybe I could even go back to school. But I don't want to stir things up for you."

My breath shot out from the very bottom of my lungs.

"He won't come back and bust in here and hit you?" I blurt out.

My mom shook her head. "The lawyers won't tell him where we live. He'd never show up in this neighborhood. The bookies around here are after him, too. Besides"—she turned her head from side to side—"I lived. See? No bruises. Hardly a scar. I'm safe now and so are you."

We weren't safe back then. Some Saturday

nights we'd find ourselves in the emergency room. Whole families paced, waiting on word about their grandpa, and then there'd be my mom and me, sitting in silence. Each time she'd tell a different story. She bumped into a wall or she fell down the stairs. There'd be stitches and ice packs and even arm slings for her cuts and sprains. But it didn't make it stop. We'd be back in a month.

My hands did something then, all by themselves. They balled up tight.

"DO IT!" I stood up, grabbing my lunch.

If I couldn't hit him, maybe the law could. *Wham!* But, running down the block to get to school on time, all I could think of was how my mom gave me one more reason to hate my dad. When we first left, my mom's cousin Yolanda took us to the shelter. But I wanted Dad back. There was something missing. We didn't have our own life anymore. We were swallowed up. At the shelter, doors slammed day and night. It had a cold feeling. We slept in a metal bed. I kicked it until my foot hurt. My mom dragged me out each morning to a new school where I never made one friend. All I wanted was my dad back. At that shelter I never felt safe. It was like I was on a long train ride, waiting for the final stop.

By the time I got to school that morning, a thunderstorm black mood had set in. It seemed like nothing would ever go right for me. In the classroom Willie catches me glaring at Destiny, the bearer of the bad news about Candees.

"She's *fass*," Willie whispers across the aisles. "Spreads *su-su*."

"What?"

"Nosy. Gossips. Don't pay her no mind!"

My mouth drops. Willie is such a quiet boy. But whenever he opens his mouth, he gets the words just right.

These women. First my mom says I am living in the past and I don't see all the good stuff right in front of me. But it's okay for Ms. Hill to talk about memories, which is living in the past. Authors she reads to us are all stuck in the past, too. Take Allen Say. When our teacher reads his book *Grandfather's Journey,* we hear how Grandfather is lonely for his homeland when he leaves it to live in America. Next Ms. Hill tricks us right then and there into a social studies lesson about our country of origin. Soon everybody is spilling stories about the places their families originally came from: Korea, Croatia, Greece, Puerto Rico, El Salvador, Italy, China.

Who cares?

"That book makes me sad," Ah Kum sighs as we take turns speaking around the circle. "I remember how my other grandmother, my dad's mom, cried when we left China. I haven't seen her for three whole years."

Destiny leans into Ah Kum, winding long strands of her friend's black hair into a braid.

"That sounds like a powerful place to write about. You can visit there with your words," suggests our teacher. "Begin with your grandmother."

Ah Kum swallows hard, holding the rest of her unspoken words inside like they burn her throat. Lin watches closely, squeezing his lips tight.

Tae Hyun's eyes widen. "I was born in Korea, but I never go back. I remember it. Lots of people and apartments. Boys and girls walk to school alone."

Ms. Hill calls on me now. In my gut, feelings

twist. My mother in shades of blue. My dad getting tracked down. The picture on the cabinet of the smiling grandparents in Puerto Rico who died before I was born. My mom's cousin Yolanda and her family are the only ones we have left. She's the reason we moved back to our old neighborhood, after circling around it so long. That, and knowing my dad would never look for us here. In fact, he'll never look for us again. I have given up on him (almost).

"Where is your family from?" Ms. Hill asks me again.

All eyes stare.

I shrug my shoulders. "The U.S.A."

The kids giggle. They eyeball one another.

Ms. Hill wears a teacher's frown if there ever was one. "I'm sure you realize by now that only Native Americans lived in this country before everyone came. Everyone is from elsewhere."

I watch Ms. Hill. She watches me. I am silent as a mummy's tomb. She takes a deep breath and extends her arm in Giovanni's direction.

"Giovanni's got a place tucked away in his head. Upstate. He can go there anytime and write about it. It's somewhere he feels strongly about. That's how people feel about the land they love."

Giovanni blushes beneath locks of his black hair. He slumps over, his chest caved in. It's like he grew too much at once and doesn't know what to do with the extra inches yet. I know he worries a lot about that book our teacher carries around. He told me if she had forty kids like Mrs. McGonigle did, she wouldn't think about us so much. He hasn't said a word in circle.

"I've got a place like that!" Willie's hand shoots up. His dreadlocks thump like wads of cotton.

No one says a word. All hands drop.

"It's hot and rolling. Hills and sea. On an island." Willie's hazel eyes spin with light. "I spend every summer there. It's where my grandma lives. In a house where you can smell the sea as soon as you wake up."

Willie pauses. He does not move and neither do we.

"Well, where is it?" Ms. Hill asks what we all wanna know.

"Oh, it's Jamaica. I have postcards of it.

The sea is a color you wouldn't believe—the lightest of blues and greens all mixed together! Like a gem in the sun."

A wave spreads across the circle. A hush.

"Do you have those postcards here?" Ms. Hill asks. Willie nods. "Paste them in your writer's notebook. Study them before you write."

Willie sits straight up and looks toward his desk. I bet he's itching to paste them in right now.

Thoughts poke me sharp as needles. *I lived in a lot of places but none of them were home. We hopped like fleas in and out of apartments when the fee went up or my dad couldn't pay the rent. We were always on the run—just like he is now. Not one was a place like Willie's. What I have to write about is things I can tell no one.*

After the shelter, we moved to a "temporary" house, as my mom kept calling it. She studied to get a nurse's aide diploma. Other families shared the kitchen and living room. It was noisy. Kind of messy, too. One mom lived there with a baby and a first grader named Billy. I took to reading out loud to block everything out. Billy crept up and listened to me

65

reading. It set him to sleep each night. He was the closest thing I had to a brother. One night that family got a phone call. Next day they disappeared. Our new housemates fought all the time. They cursed one another. My mom kept promising we'd move. Last spring, we finally moved into our studio.

The first thing I did when I got back to this neighborhood was walk the streets, checking out my dad's favorite spots: the barber; the alleyways; the park. Nobody had seen him. My mom blew a deep, long sigh. She never told me where he went, although I'd bugged her over and over again. Just gone, she said. If I had one clue, it would have been a thread tying me to him. But I didn't even have that much of him. *Poof!* Gone like smoke.

All of a sudden, something pushes up, all the way from my gut to my head.

The Edge
I stand on an edge–
not here or there.
Never knowing where I belong.
Never stayed in
one place that long.

The poem sizzles in my mind. Two words echo like a bell ringing—*belong, long*. I didn't intend it to rhyme. It just happened. I can't get it out of my head. I don't dare write it down.

THERE AND BACK AGAIN

Giovanni

I don't want any problems with Ms. Hill. So I make a deal with Mrs. Rivera. I beg her like a dog.

Per favore!
Quit haunting my desk!
I promise to do my work, so stop worrying about me.

There's a road boys like me travel on. Boys who can't do what the rest of the kids can. Read. Understand what they read. Spell. Write. My brother, Mario, went on this same road before me. He mostly went down it and not up.

When we first came to America, Mario went into a fifth grade ESL class. He barely made it. The next year, he was sent to Mrs. Rivera. She couldn't help him, she complained, because he wouldn't pay attention. But Mario swore the teacher had it in for him. "What's wrong with giggling all the time?" he argued. "Doesn't hurt nobody." Mrs. Rivera recommended him for Resource Room when he left for junior high. Hold-over letters started flying over to our house like paper airplanes. By tenth grade, the high school said they'd really have to hold him over. Mario never went back to school after that.

Once you were in Mrs. Rivera's class, you were branded, like cattle, my brother said. Mrs. Rivera was the beginning and end of the road for him. Weekdays, Mario pumps gas. Saturdays, he rolls dough for my dad in his pizza parlor. Mario plops down in front of the TV most nights, sleeps like a dead man, and stinks from gasoline. I keep my distance.

Then I get a brainstorm. Willie spoke up in circle today just like I did that time about upstate. Maybe he'll get in trouble now. It's his turn. Or Tyrone who never finishes anything. He was in Mrs. Rivera's class, too. Ms. Hill can circle their desks like a hawk after fresh prey. Here's what I figure—if I don't write too much down, she can't write as much about me. Here goes.

mistretta, sicily

i'll tell you about the one and ownly pickure i have of over their you never seen a place like it it was so green and had hills rolling up and over, up and up into the montins. The town was sleepy, sunni and hot. Narrow streets curving past poor houses. old women in black walked to the cemeterri every day. But all around it were fields of flowers and vegetables in long rows and on the hill behind my ants house was a line of skinny trees i think they are called sighpress, to mark her land.

Then I draw a picture of Mistretta, my family's hometown, while the other kids write. I draw the hills and fields and wonder how it looks compared to Willie's hills. The sea is down below. Up above, there's winding streets, houses, farms, and green.

I smell Ms. Hill's perfume. That's how I know she's getting closer. It smells like lemons and freshness. Is it fabric softener? She stops right behind me. My pencil freezes and my eyeballs roll all the way into the top of my head. Maybe she won't see me.

She nods her head at my story, then points to a circular desk by the closet. She motions for me to join her there with my notebook and pencil. It's all done in sign language, so I know I'm in trouble. Her finger is pressed over her lips. The other kids scratch away. Only Willie looks up underneath all that twisty, twirly hair. He smells it when something's up. He turns away quickly, afraid he'll be next.

I read my story aloud to the teacher. There's five periods, but, of course, she wants more. I guess where to put them. Sometimes I'm right. Sometimes I'm dead wrong.

Finally she says something. "I love how you tell your story. You use specific words that make pictures in a reader's head. You write what you know. That's what all good writers do."

In my head, I think one word: *Salute!*

"However"—Ms. Hill pauses—"there's something you need to work on."

I grab the edge of my seat and sit on my knuckles. "It's spelling, isn't it? How can I write good if I'm worried about spelling all the time?"

"Get your words down first. Don't stop writing or you'll forget the story that shines in your mind. It's hard to do two things well at the same time, kind of like passing a soccer ball while you're biking uphill. Do one thing at a time and you will get better at both."

She continues. "Point to the words you are unsure of in your spelling."

I look down. I didn't stop once this time to ask Max about spelling. I just wrote. But some look kind of twisted. I pick out one. She finds a lot more, underlining each one with her pencil. Together we use a little yellow machine, the spell-checker, to correct them.

"Type the word you wrote into this screen," she tells me.

So I do, mistakes and all. Other words pop up. She points to the best choice. At the back of my notebook, I begin my own spelling list:

Spelling Demons!
only
picture
mountains
sunny
cemetery
aunt's
cypress

"This is your personal list, Giovanni. You can add to it anytime and check it when you get stuck. It will improve your writing. Write nonstop first. Later, use the spell-check or double-check with me or Maximo."

With just one breath, my teacher gives me permission to write without worrying and talk to Maximo, too. Mrs. McGonigle never would have done that. She thought she was the only person in the whole room who knew anything. I feel relieved about where I stand with Ms. Hill. It doesn't bother me one bit when I see her writing in her black book either. She makes a little check on the page and smiles at me. I know my name's at the top. She's studying me, that's all, and she doesn't care that I can't spell.

Everything would have been all right except, at the end of the reading period, she says these words: "Class, novel studies begin next. Each of you will have your own copy of this novel. We'll read it every day in class."

Quando? I wonder.

"Tomorrow!" Ms. Hill warns as if reading my thoughts.

Scuzi!?

I am in shock. It's a chunky book with small print. It has to be way over a hundred pages. Maximo whispers he already read it at the library. He goes there every week. I never read a book the size of that one ever. Now Ms. Hill's gonna know the holy truth, and nothing but the truth about me.

THE KEY

Willie

I admit I spend most of the writing period gluing postcards down superstraight. I want to arrange them like a photo album, with pictures of Jamaica you would see when you first arrive. The airport with heat waves shimmering off the tar runway. Reggae music and humidity blasting soon as you set your feet down. Winding roads. Hills climbing up. Chicken jerky smoking the air. And peeks of aquamarine sea laughing at the sun.

I'm ready to slam my words down onto the page when—*wham!* They disappear. It's as if I crash into another player and fall straight to the pavement, the ball stolen away. Why can't I get the words down?

Something rustles in the aisles. Ms. Hill's out scouting for prey, like my mom on the track of dirty socks. The teacher let Giovanni go. I should have been on the lookout. Nearby, Destiny's pencil scrapes like lizard feet. Everything that girl does is big and noisy. I'm the opposite; I don't tell anybody anything. Well, at least we'll have quiet for a while. We won't be hearing Destiny's *chatty-chatty* voice while she speaks to her notebook with that smile on her shiny face. The teacher passes her desk by.

Ms. Hill stops right behind my desk. She sees the blank page. Who wouldn't? It's staring straight up at the both of us.

"What happened?" she asks.

My chest tightens. It's all mixed up with my grandma. We had to leave her behind again, just like every summer. But this was the very first time she didn't go to the airport with us to say good-bye. The doctor made her stay home. *Everything is* NOT *cook and curry.*

"I don't know how to begin," I tell her.

The teacher nods and jots something in this notebook she's carrying. I don't like the looks of that.

The very next day in Writers' Circle, when

she begins teaching, I know she's speaking straight to me.

"Some of you are struggling with beginnings. It's hard to know what to write down when there's so much to say. That's called a writer's block. Today, I'll show you a way to work through it before you write."

Ms. Hill calls it brainstorming. Sparks of ideas. She talks about gathering words we know will be part of our story. We just make a list of them first. She has a name for this: Key Words.

Then, she does an amazing thing. She holds one of our notebooks up and reads aloud from it. It's Giovanni's. His hair's in shock. It stands straight up like nails without any gel. He told us at lunchtime how the teacher asked him permission to share his story. We didn't believe him.

She reads:

Mistretta, Sicily

I'll tell you about the one and only picture I have of it over there. You never saw a place like it. It was so green. The hills rolled up and over, far up into the mountains. The town was sleepy, sunny, and hot.

Narrow streets curved past poor houses. Old women in black walked to the cemetery every day. But, all around it, were fields full of vegetables and flowers, planted neatly in rows. On the hill, behind my great-aunt's house, grew a line of skinny trees. I think they are called cypress. They marked her land.

All eyes swing to Giovanni. Ashley studies Gio's head like she never noticed he had a brain before. He's someone who always does goofy things to make us laugh, like play soccer with the dust balls beneath his desk. But he has a story full of pictures about his homeland and I don't.

"What were Giovanni's key words?" the teacher asks us.

Ms. Hill makes a list on the blackboard as, one by one, the words shoot out: *mountains! fields! cemetery! cypress! great-aunt's!*

Giovanni's mouth hangs down to his collar. "*Scuzi!* That's just what I was thinking before I wrote it!"

Afterward, kids burst out of the circle, sneakers squeaking across the green tiles as they hurry to their notebooks. Even Lin rushes to jot his words down in tiny Chinese letters. Around the classroom is a pulse, a beat, like drumrolls calling all pencils to write. Ms. Hill stops me in the aisle. It's the first time I stand so close to her. She's lemony-smelling. And her eyes are blue-green, the color of the sea.

"A story is a puzzle to solve," she tells me. "Try your story about Jamaica again."

On the way to my desk, words keep repeating in my head. You know how sometimes at an intersection there's a blinking yellow light? That's just how it is now. Words flash: *island and sea. Island and sea.* I make that the title in my notebook, then whip my key words down to stop them from cawing in my ears. Sweat breaks out on my neck.

grandma
heart
far away
waiting

Island and Sea

My grandma's short and skinny. Like a bone, she says. She worked in a factory all her life. She had to. My grandpa died when my mom was young so I never got to meet him. My grandma raised six kids on her own. It wore her down, my mom says, like an old mango tree with roots deep in the ground but no fruit in its arms anymore.

She had to retire last year because she had trouble breathing. The doctor says it's her heart. She walks slowly now, as if counting her footsteps. Maybe she only has so many left.

If only I could get there. But all these months of the whole school year slam down between her and me. She's waiting out there, far away, for next summer to begin, just like me. In a place of island and sea with all that water between us. No way to get across it now.

I sit straight up when I'm done. Everyone's hand is waving to share. I don't join in. Secrets just spilled onto my page and that's where I'll keep them.

DEAD-END ROAD

Destiny

That lesson about our country of origin sure was weepy. It did something to everybody. It was like an Oprah show. Max got mad—what else is new? Willie opened up wide and shared his story about his grandma in Jamaica. It was the first time he spoke in class. Asmir told us about the war in Bosnia that killed one uncle and left another missing. Natalia sat with tears filling her eyes. She did not have any stories. I wonder why. Bo Wan said she'd loan her some because her family never stops talking about the olden days in Korea.

Then Ah Kum spoke about leaving her other grandmother behind. Afterward she wrote and wrote, trying to capture what she could still remember of China and her family there. All over the margins of her notebook she drew farms, vegetable gardens, chickens, and villages. She worked in a hurry as if her pencil was leaking memories about to evaporate. I didn't share. But I wrote.

The Ancestors

If I were to try and find my country of origin, I'd have to travel every which way. It's not an easy journey or a straight one. It begins with a sad voyage all the way back to Africa aboard the ships that took us to America, that stole us away. My grandmother said the traders split black families apart, took our souls, and chained us down. That was slavery.

But we survived, my grandma said. We went on to new places. We traveled other roads.

One road would take us down south, to the cotton and tobacco plantations where my ancestors worked. Where they were given the last name I have now because it belonged to their master. He owned every part of them.

Another road went deep into the woods of South Carolina where my grandmother's great-grandpa went into hiding. He was a runaway slave and he married a Cherokee woman in the hills. We have pictures of her in front of a log cabin. She was bony with a fierce face and long skirts to the ground. She looked like a sturdy tree living out there.

After the Civil War, all the slaves were free. Many years later, their descendants began flocking like birds, one by one, to the north, to the cities, looking for work even though all they knew was farming. Most had troubles. Only some found a clear path through it.

Somehow we got to this generation. My grandma made sure my dad got his "schooling." He's a computer technician. He can fix anything with knobs from a windup toy to a Macintosh computer. Someday, he promises, we'll take a trip and go down all those roads that my grandma talks about, so we can remember where we came from. My mom's cousins laugh at the idea. Even my aunt turns her nose up at the past. I don't. I like to think that all those places make up the girl who is me. I have this feeling, too, deep inside, that I am a lot like that Cherokee woman.

Writing makes you drift and dream and say things you don't even plan on. Good thing I have a notebook to keep it private. After writing, it's back to reality.

Max is impossible to talk to. All I asked him at lunch between bites of my leftover Thanksgiving turkey with cranberry sauce and scoops of garlic stuffing is what's new at home, and he almost cussed me out. Back in class, I can't get Tyrone to tell me a thing about himself, so I gossip a little with Chelsea and Dalma. It doesn't last long because we get a reading assignment. Ashley isn't working, though. She sits with her head leaning on her hand. Her face is flushed. What's going on? Did she and Gio have a fight? There's only one way to find out. I can't help myself. I write her a note.

But Ms. Hill has her radar out. I am caught red-handed with the note between my knees.

"That's ENOUGH! This is the SECOND time!" Ms. Hill raises her voice. It frightens me. "Focus your attention on your work and not on the gossip column!"

All heads turn my way. Max smirks. Petros covers his mouth so we won't hear him giggling. Ah Kum gasps. But the worst thing is when Willie looks right at me and frowns.

Ms. Hill says I'm a busybody. Well, she didn't use that word today exactly. She's careful with her words, not like me. But that's what she means all right. It's what my dad calls me. I was dying to hear Ashley confess she was in love with Gio. She looks love struck. So does he. I just wanted to hear it from her lips first and, no, I could not wait until dismissal.

Ms. Hill has me all wrong. All I want is to be her Girl Friday, or Girl Monday, or any day she needs me, but now I have blown it. I have brushed against Ms. Hill's hard edges. I didn't know she had any.

We are at war.

DECEMBER

"I just have to show up
with my pencil."
–Willie

NOWHERE MAN

Maximo

The calendar finally rolls to the "D-Days."
That's short for December around here. Kids
count down each day to Christmas like we did
every grade so far. Even though we don't admit
we ever really believed in Santa Claus, Christmas is still the biggest holiday for fifth graders.
Everyone is waiting for something. A bike.
Rollerblades. Computer games. Music! That's
all any kid talks about.

Each day gets noisier. Mrs. Lopez complains we're like a herd of buffalo stampeding

into the lunchroom. She wears earplugs. That means we have to yell louder to get our milk. Restlessness shivers through our classroom, too. It's impossible to do math. Willie's the official snow monitor. If he sees one speck of the white stuff, he promises to spread the news immediately.

Destiny keeps asking me about my holiday plans. It's like she knows something I don't. She's always bugging me. Women do that. It's their natural instinct. I ought to know. I have one for a mom. All the teachers I ever knew were women, too. They all wanted me to do things their way, except for Ms. Hill. She and I have an understanding. She never butts in unless I'm out of line and fighting. But that Destiny. She is such a snoop! She's got no barriers and no shame either.

A blue book soon appears propped up on Ms. Hill's desk, called *Children of Christmas* by Cynthia Rylant. We all eye it.

"What's inside?" Destiny sweeps by the front of the room.

She sits right in front of the teacher's desk since last week's blowout with a substitute teacher. Destiny got caught passing a note (what else is new?) and called out twice. Her name was written on the board with three big *X*s beneath it when our teacher returned. A special log is sent home to Destiny's mom each night. Destiny gets a big check for self-control.

"Short stories" is Ms. Hill's short answer.

"*Scuzi!* The stories we write are short." Gio keeps bugging me. "Are they short stories, too?"

Finally Jackson, who now sits right beside Ms. Hill's desk since last month's report card, blurts out what we all wanna know.

"When are you gonna read it to us? It's almost Christmas!"

That very afternoon, when the sky hangs heavy with gray, and you can sniff dampness in the air, Ms. Hill carries the new book with her to the Writers' Circle. Kids step over everybody who's already seated to sit close.

"A novel is like dinner. It's a full course of characters, problems, crises, and climax," our teacher says. "But a short story is lunch. Quick. It lingers in your mind afterward. It makes you wonder about things not said."

It's all just words, I think, a teacher's speech, until she reads a short story, "Silver

Packages," from that skinny blue book. I swear there's a boy in there just like me, standing on tiptoe, waiting, his wishes and hopes secret. All I can say is it smacks you in the face by the end when the boy gets something more than he could dream of.

When the story is done, silence spreads over the circle like a sigh.

Jackson pipes up first. "Can we write about Christmas today?"

"There are many ways to respond to this story," Ms. Hill answers. "Whatever it made you think about is what to write now."

"We can choose our own topic?" Giovanni asks. Ms. Hill nods.

Tyrone grins. "I'm gonna write about what I want for Christmas."

"Presents!" Giovanni sits back, grinning.

"The trip I'm gonna take over vacation to see my cousins who moved to Virginia," Bo Wan says. "I've been waiting to go there since forever."

As usual, I don't tell mine. Back at my desk, I remember Ms. Hill recommended a word list for a writer's block, so I start with that.

All the Things I Ever Wanted
a home
a dog
grandparents
living in the same place
seeing the Mets win the World Series

My pencil stops. *Hey! I never got any of those things.* Maybe I'm just a jerk always waiting for those things to happen. I think of Gio who has fun with small stuff like dust balls. It's a good thing the school never gets cleaned much.

I add new words to my list:

my mom
best friends like Giovanni
a great class
an interesting teacher
a collection of Beatles songs

I have those things for sure. I begin a few sentences. But what I'm writing isn't what I really want to say. Across the room, Ms. Hill's pencil slides smoothly across the page. She has a little smile, too, like she's happy with the ideas pouring out. But my words are dull and don't go anyplace. I want my writing to have the same energy as that short story.

But something is in the way. Something is always in the way. . . . *I never expected it. When I came home from school yesterday, my mom was humming, wearing her bright new clothes. It was her day off. Something was up. She's been smiling more. So strange, after telling me about tracking my father down. It's like something lifted off her. It sure didn't lift off me. I've been stuck in neutral, waiting for the bad news. Then we had another talk. Then I knew. Nothing will ever be the same again. . . .*

Most kids are done writing when Ms. Hill passes by my desk. She's a fountain of lemon fabric softener, like Giovanni says. She notices my stalled pencil.

I sit real still while she studies me. I remember the poem that came out of nowhere before, how I didn't want to write it down for anyone to see. But the words popped out of me anyway.

"Can I just write how I feel?" I look up. "No story or anything?"

She nods. "Writers often write about their personal feelings."

12/6 Nowhere Man

My mom and I have a collection of old Beatles songs. One of the songs that always sticks in my head is "Nowhere Man." Imagine telling everyone you're a loser? That's just what the Beatles do. Only they are somebody, and famous, too, so you know it's just a passing moment for them.

All the other kids buzz about their holiday plans. Grandma's house. Presents from their brothers and sisters. Feasts all day long. Know what I'm getting? My mom has to work Christmas Day. I'll be on my own. Sure, I'll spend the afternoon with my cousins. But it's not the same as spending that one magical morning with your own family, in your own home, awakening to presents.

New Year's Eve at Yolanda's place is our big night out. Except this year, my mom invited a friend. Tom. He's a physician's assistant who works in the nursing home on Tuesdays. "You'll like him. All the patients adore him," she tells me, her face lit up like birthday candles. But she uses that same tone when she hands me yucky cough medicine. He's the reason behind the new clothes. The two of them already went out on a date. Whenever the phone rings now, I won't answer it. It'll be Tom.

My mom is changing without me. She's leaving me behind.

I've got nothing and nowhere and no one, same as the Beatles. But I wouldn't let anybody in on it. Just my notebook. It stays right here, between me and the page. Nobody will get this out of me, not even my mom.

By the time I finish, it's the middle of a math lesson. I am the first one to see it. Snowflakes! Faster and faster they fall down. They are the perfect kind to cover the sidewalks and cushion our slides on the way home.

Willie's dreadlocks twirl. It's as if he's reading my mind.

"Snowballs!" he mouths to me.

That's the end of work for us that day.

NO WAY

Giovanni

A novel is not like dinner. It's more like a chunk of cardboard. There's no way you can chew your way through that stuff. Whatever Ms. Hill teaches blows in and out of my head like hot air. No matter how many times I hear those fancy words, I cannot get them straight. What do *crisis* and *climax* and *problem* have to do with a book anyway? It's me who's got problems. I can't read.

Non capisco!

Soon, the teacher promises, we will read a book about the wilderness. Why can't we talk about it, or better yet just go upstate and see it? Why do we have to r-e-a-d about it?

Then I remembered my November report card. It popped up last month like a germ threatening to take me over. The hold-over box was checked of course. There were ten Ns. I got Es in attitude and respect. And a note about my enthusiasm. My mom went to see Ms. Hill at a parent-teacher conference with my aunt.

"It's good and bad news," my aunt said when they got back.

"What's the good news?"

"You're not getting worse. In fact, you got your first Es ever."

"What's the bad news?"

"Your teacher explained how she had to give the HO letter. It's not a fortune-teller's prediction or anything. The principal made her. She didn't want to do it. The district says if last year's score was too low, they must send one out."

"But what about this year?" I look at my mother.

"You're gonna pass if you improve in reading."

Soon I am back at the circular table with Ms. Hill again. Only this time, I am not alone. All the ESL kids are with me. Non-English-speaking kids fill the school. One ESL teacher teaches them all. She visits each group twice a week. The rest of the time, they stay in class. So our teacher decides to make a new reading group—the bottom reading group. Everyone's face is flushed. Lin. Tae Hyun. Ramneet and Carmen. While the rest of the class does charts of the novel's crisis and climax and draws scenes, our group is swallowing hard at the back of the room. It's all a blur to me. I don't even remember the name of our book. I drift.

Way back in first and second grade, when I

first came to PS 1, I was in ESL. When I finally passed the ESL test, I thought I would fly through life. That's when my real troubles began. I was expected to know how to read the very next day. Nobody taught me how. I only had word lists we had to copy, lines we chanted like a song. I never had trouble saying them. But no one told me what they meant.

No matter how hard I try to push my brain to work now, it doesn't matter. There's a big black mark against my name—the HO threat.

Mi sono smarrito! is all I can think.

Suddenly Ms. Hill's voice interrupts me. She points to vocabulary words written on a big white chart.

"*Wandering,*" Ms. Hill reads, looking around the circle. "The boy is *wandering* around the city looking for the house. What does that word mean?"

Carmen and Ramneet quickly bow their heads and study their fingernails for dirt. Lin is off the hook. He says only one word in English now. It's *hello.*

"Giovanni?"

My stupid head is the only one sticking up.

"Umm . . . Going around, maybe?"

"That's a start," the teacher says. "Does the boy find what he's looking for?"

She wants something more from me.

"Lost!" Tae Hyun suddenly announces.

We all stare at him. He saves us!

Then we begin reading aloud about the wandering boy, each of us taking turns around the circular table. Ms. Hill keeps interrupting the story, asking questions that stick in the way like a big STOP sign. Teachers always ruin the story that way. I don't answer any questions. Soon I'm way lost like the character in the story.

It's my turn to read, but I can't find my place. I don't even think I'm on the right page. Where is Max when I need him? I try to see where Carmen's finger is but she's across from me and her book is upside down. Then I peek sideways at Tae Hyun. His fingers are plastered on top of page 41 holding the words down like he's afraid they'll run away.

I mumble my way through the paragraph. Ms. Hill asks me to tell her more about the wandering boy. I wish I had paid attention to the words. Instead, I was thinking about last night, when my dad came home late. My brother was stretched out on the couch watching TV, his T-shirt hanging out of his pants. My dad tapped him on the head and sighed. "What am I gonna do with you, Mario? You're going nowhere." Those words echoed in my head all night long. My dad didn't say one word about my report card. He had to know. He signed the report card, too.

A strange wave of heat blows nearby. The temperature is rising in Tae Hyun's body. His big black eyes are fixed right on me. He looks trapped. Suddenly I realize that he wants me to come up with the right answer even more than I do. His turn is next! If I figure out this part, he's got a chance with the next paragraph.

I open my mouth, but, suddenly, I feel a chill. Up in the air, above our heads, Mrs. Rivera circles us with a red pen in her hand.

"Wrong! Wrong! Wrong!" she shouts.

I begin to sneeze like crazy. I duck low in my seat, out of Mrs. Rivera's way. I remember she had black circles beneath her eyes and wore the same few dresses over and over. She leaned real close, so I couldn't breathe. I never opened my mouth because Mario swore it would be worse if I did. "Don't ever answer!" he warned me. "She's just waiting to catch you like a mouse in her trap."

A light pops into Ramneet's eyes as he explains everything to Ms. Hill. It's a miracle. All the ESL kids sigh. My body is one long breath.

Tae Hyun reads next. He halts after every word, pronounces sounds oddly with a round mouth, but his voice is loud and clear. He just keeps going ahead, no matter what he sounds like. That boy sure is determined. He gets in trouble only when Ms. Hill pins him down with those questions of hers. Then his face turns watermelon pink. Words jam in his throat like dry toast. If you look in his eyes, you know he understands the story. But the words can't find the way to his lips yet.

12/8 No way

If i don't find a new rode to reading, i'm gonna be sitting hear all next year in fifth grade. Max and Willie will go ahead without me. They'll leave me behind.

I'm gonna fail. i just know it.

96

STRAY BOY

Willie

We have gym once in a while. It's always getting canceled because someone's using the gym or it's raining outside. But mainly it's because there's usually another citywide test to study for instead. Our daily schedule announces: Test Prep! Test Prep! Little booklets passing our way to make us think double quick and bubble in answers to beat the ticking timer.

Today, nothing gets in the way. We leap down the stairs into the yard for a soccer game.

"Scuzi!" Giovanni runs up to me. "Pass it to me!"

He's all over the yard like a roadrunner, slipping and sliding with the ball. He even falls on his backside. My belly aches from laughing. Before we know it, Max joins us. We divide into teams, the three of us against Mohammed, Asmir, and Jackson. Jackson's short but he's wild. Sometimes he lies down on top of the ball or stuffs it beneath his shirt. Once he jumped on my back just as I was passing to Max. Jackson never heard of soccer rules.

"Yellow card!" our referee, Petros, shouts at him ten times.

If this were a real game, Jackson would be out permanently.

When the bell rings, I lean against the fence to catch my breath. Giovanni and Max whirl in circles. Gio doubles over, cut in half with laughs like waves that do not stop. Max balances like a circus dog twirling with the soccer ball on his nose. His usual deadpan face cracks up. The two of them don't mind losing. They join the lineup, laughing so loud that Ms. Hill blows the whistle at them. I am left on my own again.

Back in the classroom, we settle down to math. We spend last period in Writers' Circle, usually my favorite, but not today. If only Ms. Hill hadn't read another short story, "Stray," from Cynthia Rylant's *Every Living Thing*. I swear nobody breathed during the reading. Dalma kept her head down the whole while. Natalia looked frozen stiff. Ashley's cheeks turned as red as her hair. I thought she was going to cry.

I don't have to tell you it was sad. A stray dog wants to be inside. The girl wants to keep the stray. Both of them have holes in their lives. Neither one has a true family. Each one hopes on the other one. All of us were thinking, "Oh no! How's this ever gonna work out?" I even caught Jackson crossing his fingers.

All my life I've been a stray. If you asked me where home was, I couldn't answer right away. New York is where my mom can make good money as a registered nurse. She came here to finish her education. My aunts and cousins are spread out over the five boroughs like pigeon peas in a plate of rice. We all have our feet in two countries. But it's so cold here in the city. Winter days are bitter and damp, unless I heat up juggling a soccer ball. Summer seems far away, along with my grandma in Jamaica.

Something always calls me away.

Things changed in our family from the way it was supposed to be. My dad drifted away from us one day and never came back. I was a little kid then. I wasn't important enough to keep him with us, I thought. But my aunts say my dad drifted all his life. I wanted to prove them wrong, believing he'd come back for me, instead of leaving me with a family full of women's chatter.

The only one who understands me is my grandma. We look alike. We're skinny—*maga,* Grandma says. Same pointy chin. Crooked little grins. The way our memories rise up, like thick fog clouding a good sunny day. Perhaps it's the past that sits on her chest like a heavy weight. Is that why she can't breathe good? If only she'd stand up high enough, on her tippy toes, so she could see the sea, everything would be just fine. Only she'd smile and say, *"Everything cook and curry!"* And it would be, too. That's how the wide sea makes you feel.

Beside me, Max slouches in Writers' Circle. I am more like him than he knows. Maybe that's why we both get along with Gio. He makes us crack up. It makes us forget everything. After Ms. Hill dismisses us to write, I walk silently to my desk.

12/14 Memory

My grandma says I think too much. The day my dad left us, walking to town with his suitcase, she dragged me down to the beach. I screamed all the way. I wanted to follow my dad to town instead. That way, I thought, he'd have to come back. I was five years old.

"No one worries by the sea, chil'," my grandma taught me then. "The sea going to roll your *crosses* 'round and 'round. Carry them far away. You left walking free as air."

She turned my head away from the road so I had to look straight ahead at the sea. Light blue danced inside the dark blue waves. Teal fish were running right through it. The roar of the surf pounded in my ears like a heartbeat. Everything came alive right in front of me.

"You *eased-up* now, Willie?" she asked me.

In my story, when I hit the painful stuff, the part about when my dad left, it was like one high wave crashing over me. But I kept on writing. The wave passed. My words found their home. I just have to show up with my pencil. Jamaica's inside me. I can go there anytime, like Ms. Hill told Gio. I don't have to wait and wait.

I stretch up when I'm done to see the windows are a white blur. Big snowflakes fall down in slow motion. The air is thick with them. My head swivels around. I look straight at Max. Our eyes lock. I catch him in the exact moment he notices the snow. The biggest grin spreads over his face. We are on the same wavelength. Finally! It's the first time I made him smile. He could be my *main man*!

HOW TO CATCH A POEM

Destiny

I'm not going into detail about my new seating arrangement. Let's just say I don't have much of a view except the blackboard. My desk is flat against Ms. Hill's on an island with no row attached. I keep twisting around to see what everyone's up to. OUCH! My neck hurts.

The one advantage is a close-up of Ms. Hill. Sometimes I see her doodling in her plan book. Shhh! There's more. I even catch her daydreaming, studying the maple tree the way Willie does. Can teachers drift and dream? Do they think about other things besides math and writing and students who don't do their work? This one sure does.

Wish I could go back to my own seat. Why can't I be sweet and contained like Ah Kum? She knows, for instance, that Ashley has fallen bad for Gio, Willie can't do math, and that Max must have had a fight at home. She heard it from me first that Natalia was adopted, and did not know her grandparents' country of origin, and how confused she feels. But Ah Kum doesn't blab to anybody. I broadcast the news like the morning newspaper, my dad jokes. I can't help it. Whatever I think flies out my mouth in the same second. Not Ah Kum. She takes everything in with those black eyes of hers that are as deep as secret treasure caves. There's a million stories glistening in her eyes if you just have time to look.

My Best Friend

My dad calls Ah Kum "a little lady." She watches her tongue. She's a deep thinker. I can half guess what her life is like. She never invites me over to her place. She always comes to my home or meets me at the library. Loads of relatives squeeze into her small apartment—her grandparents, an uncle or two, her parents, and three older brothers. Her lunch is leftover stir-fry with bean cakes for dessert that her grandmother neatly packs in Tupperware. The two of them stroll arm in arm to PS 1 every day. They wear shy little smiles and never speak.

The first time I met Ah Kum was the day I read Frog and Toad in first grade. I looked up and knew

that's what we would be—best friends forever—
even though we are so different. Each school morning it takes her at least a half hour to smile at me.
By the end of the day, she's blooming, her face pink
and flushed with laughter. Until her dad arrives to
meet her. Then the flower that is Ah Kum closes up.

Once I caught her crumpling up a math test with
a 95 percent on it. That would go right up on my re-
frigerator. Not in Ah Kum's house. She said she
must get 100 percent plus all the bonus questions,
too. Her dad wants her to be a pharmacist. Ah Kum
wants to read novels, dye her hair auburn, and be
an artist.

Please make me a little like Ah Kum. Nobody's happy with me the way I am. Whatever
it is Ms. Hill wants for me, I want it, too. If she
wants us to become poems, let it happen to
me, like it's happening in bits and pieces to
Willie, Gio, Ah Kum, and Jackson. I'm always
spouting lyrics anyway. I memorize all my favorite songs. That way, if any rap star calls me
up, I'll be ready to represent them. Knowing
their work inside out will be my first test.

Soon I find myself on the rug for the writing
lesson, snuggling up to Ah Kum. I am so happy

to be off my island and have company, that I am all ears for the lesson on how to write a poem. My grandma says that in her day, she learned the three Rs: Reading, wRiting, and aRithmetic. Wait until she hears what Ms. Hill's up to now. She's teaching the three Rs but they're way different.

They're poems.

Our teacher copies lines on the blackboard from the picture book *Fireflies*. She asks us to guess the three Rs of poetry. I remember reading that book in second grade, then drawing a hundred yellow lights on black construction paper. They were like tiny lanterns shining in the dark.

Fireflies!
Blinking on, blinking off,
dipping low, soaring high above my head,
making circles around the moon,
like stars dancing.

"A beat!" Amber sways from side to side. She's in my dance class.

"WOW, it's got rhythm!" I shout.

"What else gives it rhythm?" Ms. Hill asks.

"I see a pattern," Ashley says. "Three syllables. Then three more. 'Blink-ing-on.' Then 'blink-ing-off.' Then 'dip-ping-low.'"

"Very good!" Ms. Hill looks surprised.

"Rhyme!" Jackson shouts.

"No!" Angel tells him. "There's lots of 'ing' words, but no rhymes."

"*Scuzi!*" Gio blurts out. "Opposites!"

We check the lines. He's right: on-off, low-high. That kind of makes the words swing back and forth. But there's another R. What is it?

"Repeating lines! . . . Blinking on! . . . Blinking off!"

Willie and Max scream it out together, standing up. If they were side by side, there'd be high fives.

"You guessed the three Rs!" Ms. Hill smiles. "Rhythm. Rhyme. Repetition. Secrets to a good poem."

The class buzzes. A hum passes from desk to desk. We all want to write our own poem now. Ms. Hill says all you have to do is read a poem, and soon a beat will play in your head and drive you so crazy, you'll have to write the words down just to get rid of them. That makes us laugh. We'd love it if words rushed by that easy, tickling our brain.

There's a song inside me that began with reading about the fireflies.

Tap! Tap! Tap! The words snap.

Shivers ripple through my belly like butter-flies. It builds, lifting up to my chest, like wings fluttering across my heart. Something's going to happen. My pencil glides across the page as if I didn't own it.

What's a Poem?
A poem does not sit
flat on a page.
It lifts up
to dance and sing along
with the music
in your head.
A poem is
quarter notes and full beats
tapping
in your brain.
A poem is not a poem.
It's a song
you sing.

Whew! I never had a day quite like this. My brain hurts from all the tapping. So do my fingers. I wring out my hands. Then I draw tiny fireflies soaring all around my poem.

Poems arrive like fireflies blinking at you in the middle of darkness. Surprises. You've got to grab them quick before they fly off. I'm sure glad I caught this one.

JANUARY

"Make the words mine,
one at a time."
—Giovanni

WHEN I WAS YOUNG

Maximo

During Christmas vacation, I like to stay wrapped in my down comforter as long as I can. Curled up, sleepy as a slug, unwilling to wake up in the half dark, crisp, cold mornings. But for the first time in my whole life, I ran back to PS 1 when school reopened that January. *Slam! Bang! Pound!* My feet hit the sidewalk. No, we did not have a white Christmas. New York never does. That wasn't the reason. It was because there was nothing to play with except the thoughts circling in my head.

How could I forget New Year's Eve at Yolanda's? We took turns banging on my cousin Jose's new drums. We beat them to the Beatles, Aretha Franklin, Celia Cruz, and Christmas hymns. Every kid screamed and sang along. It was so hot in Yolanda's apartment, we opened the windows wide and the door, too. Our music joined in with all the voices calling and laughing from all the other apartments. Neighbors walked in and out. The building was one big indoor party like Gio's house. The adults danced and we ordered Chinese food.

That was the good part.

Back here, in 5E, it's a brand-new year. A place to try being someone else. My no. 2 pencils are sharp. I want to forget all about my life, but Destiny's face is in mine, asking what I think of Tom, and guess what else? Ms. Hill wants us to look back. She reads another memoir, Cynthia Rylant's *When I Was Young in the Mountains*. Everyone loves that author. Not me. When the other kids remember their childhood, there's a glow over everything. Ramneet's face softens when he tells us about first seeing snow fall in New York City the day he arrived from Delhi, India.

It's not like that for me.

How can I capture what it was like when I was young? I blocked it out. *Wham!* I slammed a wall down between me and the past. Whole years are a blur. *Who taught me my first word? Did my dad ever carry me when I was a baby? Why can't I remember?*

Over the vacation I found out why I had no memory. Better to be blank than know the truth. My mom finally had a day off. We unpacked our boxes. Books. The down comforter, thank goodness. Out tumbled Yolanda's letter to my mom begging her to leave "for Max's sake." My mom handed me a manila envelope stuffed with old photos.

"I wanted to rip them up. But I kept them . . . for you."

We looked through them without a word. In one picture my mom held me, a newborn. Long hair covered half her face, so you couldn't see her eyes. I turned my head to study her beside me. She looked younger now with her ruby lipstick and bright T-shirt. A picture of my dad and me popped up next. I was two, standing next to him, my hands balled up tight. He didn't look back at my mom holding the camera but stared way off, probably watching for his friends. Even though we had the same pug noses and straight hair, I knew something way back then—he never wanted us. Most of the time, I kept five steps back from him, in case I had to run.

I'm trying my best to forget everything now. But it still happens that I see things I don't like. Maybe if I stick it in a memoir, the words will get stuck on the page instead of just inside me.

1/02 Happy New Year

New Year's Eve was not quiet. It was more like *The Relatives Came* than *When I Was Young in the Mountains.* None of us did any thinking, just eating and making noise. Drums, horns, and loud music. That's what you're supposed to do on New Year's Eve, Bo Wan says—bang pots and make loud sounds to chase evil spirits away and bring in the new year.

Tom told a lot of doctor jokes that made everyone laugh (not me). He's a foot taller than my mom, with wheat-colored curly hair and freckles everywhere, even on his arms. He had to bend down to look at my mom. He inspected her closely like she was a delicate china cup in an antique shop.

And it would have been all right. It would have been fine except for the kiss.

When the countdown began, my mom and Tom were twirling slowly even though the music in the background was heavy metal. Then the ball dropped. Everyone leaped up. Jose shot confetti in the air. Another kid blew on a party horn right into my ear. I turned to my mom and Tom. The two of them made a kind of circle. The air around them was different. Hushed. Then the circle closed. He leaned in and kissed her.

I don't remember my mom and dad kissing. Ever! There was always a crackle in the air. Static. My mom's face always pale, sometimes a purple bruise beneath her eye. My dad sat for hours staring at the television, while I'd only half do my homework, and my mother silently did her chores, our breaths on hold, waiting for the quiet to snap. Even after my dad left, and we had a kind of boring quiet, I listened for something to break. To ruin it again. I still do. Like how I'm waiting now, on hold, to hear from him.

What does it mean when a boy kisses a girl? It's nothing they say aloud. I think it's a secret between the two of them, kept spinning inside their circle where they let no one in.

I wonder where all those feelings go, once the circle breaks.

It's not forever. I already know that.

NO PROBLEMS PLEASE

Giovanni

I am saved. Finally, the ESL teacher arrives to pick up all the ESL kids. The only free time she has to teach them happens to be during our reading group.

"Half the school is ESL," she says to Ms. Hill. "The borough of Queens is like the United Nations."

When the ESL kids line up to leave with her, a dark shadow trails behind them out the door. Can it be Mrs. Rivera? I sure hope so. I did beg my old reading teacher to leave that one time, but she didn't seem to be listening.

I stay with the class when they begin Gary Paulsen's *Hatchet*. That's the book Maximo keeps talking about. He picked it up at the library last summer and read it straight through. It took a whole afternoon, he said. All the while, his heart never stopped thumping.

We don't get far into reading this book aloud

when I'm perching on the edge of my seat like a bird ready to take off. The main character reminds me of Max. He's a boy on his own, too. Max goes home to an empty apartment, he tells me. Nobody cooks except on his mom's day off. He doesn't have much family either. I study my friend as the words spill over the air. I see why he liked the book now.

But then, something else happens. A feeling builds. It starts like a little worry pumping in my veins, but, soon enough, my heart races like I'm running down the block. This is *the problem*!!!! It's got to be. My hair stands straight up like electricity. I only get that when there's big trouble in my house.

"How does the boy feel about his life? What are his problems when the book begins?" Ms. Hill asks us. "What terrible new problem appears at the end of the chapter?"

There's that word again. *Problem.* The kids start a discussion, but I can't listen. Instead, I worry about that poor boy. He's alone with no one to help. What would I do in his place? My life is easier than his, is my first thought. I would not want to be in that boy's place. I'd take my house any day for the situation he's in.

Funny, that's just what Ms. Hill asks us to write down in our notebooks: Compare and contrast your life with this boy's life.

1/15

The boy and i both have problems but his life is an emeergenci. Mine is just nosey. Anyone can live with that. I'd get out of that plane or do something if i were him.

He's alone. Sometimes I feel alone too. My brother makes fun of me. My mom can't help me with my homework because she has trouble reading English. My dad is not home much so he can't pay attenshun to me. I worry I won't make it to the next grade.

The boy remembers bad stuff. I don't. The memory of Sicily popped out of me. I didn't know it was there, deep down. The boy discovers how to save himself. It was there inside him all along. Is the secret to learning to read inside me too? Something i have to discover? It can't be something only certain kids get, and not me. Maybe you have to want it bad. Maybe you have to be in a despurrate situation, like the boy was. Like me, the only boy who can't read. Maybe you have to ask for it to come. Pay attenshun and sit still. Then it will rise up like a bone some dog buried so long ago, they don't even remember it.

My only hope is Max. Reading is like breathing to him. I'm gonna study him, watch how he does it so i can do it too.

So I invite Max to my dad's pizza place one day after school. It's called Gloria's Pizza (named after my mom). My dad makes the best thin-crusted pizza around. He rolls it just right. He's got great hands, like my grand-parents. His dad was a baker back in Sicily and his mom was a seamstress. His sauce has secret ingredients. Deep red with a dash of oregano, fresh basil, and heavy on the garlic. You can order toppings like sausage, olives, and mushrooms, too.

Max is all eyes when we get to Gloria's. It's steamy inside from all the cooking, with a heat that thaws your toes even inside your boots. Max steps right up to the counter. You can't stand there long without doing two things— whipping your jacket off, and ordering your slice. Soon Max and I are sitting down at a booth in our T-shirts, swallowing hot pizza. My friend has a ring of red sauce around his grin.

"Hey, Gio, this is some mozzarella cheese. Look! I can stretch it like a rubber band from my slice to yours, and back across the table again. Sure beats peanut butter and jelly. Can we get some more?"

Then in walks Anna Marie for a slice. She just stepped off the subway from her school in Manhattan with a tote bag full of fabrics. The rest of my grandparents' talent flowed into my sister's hands. Whenever she goes shopping, she feels fabrics, and smooths them over and over. She studies them like art. Sometimes she falls in love with a dress in Bloomingdale's. She'll talk nonstop about it. Then she'll sketch it. My mom yells at her for stepping into that fancy store.

"We can't even afford underpants in Bloomingdale's!"

But my sister is not a dreamer like me. She's a schemer. She'll haunt the garment district for a fabric with perfect drape, and then sew that same Bloomingdale's dress out of thin air. No book to tell her how. It's there in her hands.

"Hiya, Gio." Anna Marie slides in next to me. "Who do you have here with you?"

"Max. He's my new friend in Ms. Hill's class."

"Nice hair, Max. Where do you get it done?"

Max blushes. I never saw him do that before. He doesn't know what to say. You have to meet my sister to understand she really wants to know. She picks up tips from everyone on style. So I elbow him for an answer.

"Ah . . . the Greek barber right around the corner from here," he says.

My sister nods her head of dark brown curls, set with gobs of gel, chews her slice, then takes out a pair of needles and begins to knit a fuzzy, itchy, mohair sweater. Max sneezes. That's the end of the conversation.

Here I thought I would learn Max's secret recipe for reading, but instead, after we filled our bellies, we both watched my dad work. Maybe it was because Max has no dad that got me thinking. I finally got it—there's nowhere he can go to see his.

1/22 Gloria's pizza

Wen my dad works, he talks on the phone, holding it to one ear with his shoulder to take an order.

One hand stirs sause, while the other hand checks the ovens. He's like an octopus, doing so many things at once.

he doesn't like to dress up. Mostly he wears a wite undershirt because it's hot by the ovens. Flour dots him up and down. Sometimes, his thick, black hair turns white. He never stops to dust himself off.

wen Max looks at that space where a dad should be, someone to turn his way, there's no one there. No one. My dad may not be home much, but, at least he's there. He's my hero. He saved many years to come to New York. He's the first one in our family to own his own busyness in America. I wanna be just like him.

Here's what I'm most afraid of. Something i never told anybody. Maybe I'll never learn how to read. my dad will tap my head someday too and tell me I'm going nowhere like Mario. i don't know if I'll be able to lift myself up to the plase where my dad is waiting for me to be. Maybe he'll give up on me like Max's dad did.

I've got to find a way to read. If Willie and Max do it, it can't be so terrible. There's got to be something I can do to catch up. Reading with the rest of the class continues, but it gets stranger. Each day Ms. Hill writes questions on a chart for us to think about:

How do the boy's problems make you feel?
What does it remind you of?
What other book can you compare this to?
What more do you want to know about this situation?

I stare at the chart. *Scuzi?* Nobody asked me these questions before. Does Ms. Hill actually want to know what I think? Isn't a story something all wrapped up like a present? Our teacher hints that a story can be alive, that it can change because of what readers think. It can change us, too, she says.

"Psst!" I hiss at Max, who is busy writing.

He slides his eyes my way.

"Do you still go to the library?" I ask him. He nods.

"Can you . . . take me?"

Our eyes meet. I've asked him plenty of stupid stuff, but never this.

"When?" he wants to know.

"When are you going?"

"Saturday. My mom and I will pick you up."

On Saturday I awaken early. My dad is already gone to Gloria's, dragging along my sleepy-headed brother. I don't eat breakfast, not even the chocolate *brioche*. My mom feels my forehead to see if it's hot.

Outside, I see Max waving. I run out. His mom is skinny, dresses like a teenager, but without the makeup and highlighted hair. Dark circles hang beneath her eyes. But when she smiles, all her tiredness disappears.

"Hi, Giovanni!" She shakes my hand. "Max talks about you all the time. You are the only person who can make him laugh. I can't even get him to do that."

Max smiles at me and swings his books up in the air.

In the library everyone bustles in and out. There's a long line to check out, same as Key Food. Only it's quiet. You can almost hear people thinking. Old men lean over newspapers. Kids grab DVDs. Asians crowd into one aisle full of books printed in their languages. There's so many books I never heard of. I bet there's a million. Most look dog-eared, with worn covers.

By the CDs, Bo Wan and her sisters wave

at us, headphones on. Then Jackson and his cousin rush over. They point out Vinny the Hammer reading in the Adult section. We jump up and down at the sight of him. He leans against the stacks, wearing sweatclothes, his eyes stuck on his book. We wanna rush right over and beg him for his autograph. Or ask him to pose for a left hook. But Max insists you cannot interrupt someone famous who is daydreaming beneath a bookshelf titled "Poetry." It might be embarrassing.

Everyone is searching for something, I guess.

I peek in the section marked Young Adult where a whole top shelf is loaded with Gary Paulsen's books. There's one copy of *Hatchet*. I grab it. Max promises not to tell me the ending. He picks *Brian's Winter*, a sequel, and tucks it under his armpit along with *Canyons*, another Paulsen. While we wait in the forever checkout line, we both reread the second chapter of my book together, right on the spot.

The words are still lighting up my mind like a billboard when the librarian hands me my first ever library card. The Queens Borough Public Library, it says. It's plastic, with code numbers drilled on it like a credit card. When I sign my name on the back, I feel rich. Suddenly, I am somebody who reads.

Did you ever hug a book? I do. All the way home. Even though it's borrowed, it seems like mine. I'll own it for three whole weeks. Anytime I want, I can peek inside. Sneak in a few pages. Take my time. I won't have to hurry my way through it like in class.

As soon as I'm home, I hide it beneath my pillow. I don't want my brother to catch me reading.

"Books are the enemy!" he yelled at me once. "So are teachers. There's other things to know."

Scuzi? I wanted to snap back at Mario. Like what—waking up when it's dark to pump gas by the expressway until you come home stinking of it? Or not being able to buy the motorcycle you dream about for two whole years even if you saved every penny (which you don't)?

But I am too polite to say it, and, besides, there'd be a major war if I did. I have to share a room with Mario. So let me just slip beneath the covers with my dad's flashlight and beam it on this book until my brother comes home. Read it slowly, letting it last like hard candy. Make the words mine, one at a time.

WARM-UP

Willie

It's chilly out. Ms. Hill asks me to crack the windows open an inch to disinfect the classroom air. Flu germs hide everywhere, she whispers. The teacher has no voice. Giovanni barks like a hound dog. Ashley's nose is as bright as her hair. Five empty desks sit ghostlike for many January days.

"Willie, I'm a little worried about you." The teacher hands me the tall window pole. "Your writing is beginning to sparkle, but, lately, you seem daydreamy again, like back in September. Is anything wrong?"

It's impossible to look at Ms. Hill and lie. Those blue eyes of hers are wide open like the sea, searching inside of me.

"It's my grandma. . . . She . . . she's in the hospital."

I swallow hard. There's that tightening in my chest again, the squeezing down and trying not to cough. I tell her about Christmas. The days waiting to hear the news. The calls to intensive care. We found out that my grandma had a heart attack.

"She won't be coming home for a while. My family can't visit her either. No one can afford time off from work."

"Did you get to talk to her?"

"Just for a few minutes on New Year's Day. Her voice was low. It never is. You can hear my grandma yell all the way down to the beach. She said she'd see me when the mangoes ripen this summer."

"She sounds like a strong woman, Willie. I am sure she'd like to hear from you again. It's a long way to summer. Why don't you write her a letter?"

All the noise in the room dims. Nothing seems to move, not even the clock.

"What . . . what would I say?"

"You're a good writer. Tell her something to make her smile."

All that day, I wonder about what Ms. Hill said. A cloud settles over my head. Part of me is sitting at my desk, but the best part floats away. I aim my pencil at the page, but nothing happens. Destiny shows up at my elbow, her face shining like a fat coffee bean. Her eyes sparkle, making me want to listen. She talks fast, her arms flying in the air. She doesn't want to borrow anything. She brings an idea.

When the teacher calls us to join her in the Writers' Circle, we huddle together. We want a story to heat us up. We're all done with *Hatchet* and hoping for another Gary Paulsen book. But Ms. Hill has other shells to pry open, as my grandma says.

"Writers don't use boring words like *nice, great, happy, wonderful,* and *a lot.* Those words don't put pictures in our heads. Specific words do."

Whaddup? Our mouths have that hangdog look again.

"Specific words sparkle. They are words that make you feel things in your heart and see things close up. They are the details that pull you into the story. Let's listen for them now."

Ms. Hill reads a story after all. The lesson has been a warm-up for "Grandmother's Kitchen" from a book called *Home*. It's a little one-page description, a memoir, a looking back. Cynthia Rylant remembers her grandma's tiny kitchen where everybody from cousins to aunts and uncles sits around with her grandma, eating and telling stories. We find the specific words right away:

angel food cake
Coca-Cola
oak table
hollow

Soon Gio is giving the recipe for his grandmother's garlic meatballs, and Carmen is remembering spicy black beans with pork. Lin smiles when Ah Kum talks about shrimp chow fun. But I am smelling chicken jerky smoking all the way down the hill as my cousins and I run out of the pounding waves. I'm uphill, almost touching the mango tree in my grandma's yard. I am getting hungrier by the minute.

I don't stop to talk on the way back to my desk. I grab a piece of loose-leaf instead of my notebook. My mind is a sharp pencil tip.

Dear Grandma,
I will be there when the mangoes are *fit*. How could I miss that? They're my favorite fruit, yours

too. I remember how sometimes a plump mango falls down from your tree when it's heavy and ready to eat. Plop! It scares my little cousins as much as your *duppy* stories.

Soon you'll sit outside under the wide open arms of that mango tree. Someone will be *jerking* chicken in the kerosene pan. Neighbors will come by with hot *bammy.* All my aunts and cousins will arrive sweating and laughing from New York with piles of luggage. We will have a *run a boat.* There will be shade in the summer, sea breezes, and fresh coconut milk. I can't wait to get there.

Your faithful grandson,
Willie

I know why writers write—they write to untangle the knots in their hearts. It makes *everything cook and curry* again.

ESP

Destiny

You'd think a vacation would do everybody good. Not these 5E boys. Max's edge is sharper than ever. Even holidays make him uptight. Gio, who is always so sweet, grabs

Gary Paulsen's *The River* right out of my hands. I had just found it in our class library and shouted the news when he leaps out of his seat like Superman to snatch it. No apology and no thank-you either. Just straight to his seat to read it. Then there's Willie. He looks thinner. He slumps like a water-logged noodle in his seat as if something is pressing down on him.

Only Ms. Hill looks brand new. Her nails are a lot longer for one thing. Amber says they're acrylic and estimates they're the $45.00 kind. But there's something I just can't put my finger on. Sometimes she smiles to herself like she's listening to a joke in her head. Her face is flushed. She's the only one in the room who looks like she's having fun. There's got to be a reason. She can't be our teacher and look so happy. Is she in love?

One cold afternoon we run back from the gym all sweaty after relay races. As soon as we sit down in the classroom, Willie starts coughing. He can't stop. His face squeezes tight as he pulls hard for a breath. Ms. Hill opens the windows while Mohammed hunts for Willie's inhaler in his desk. Willie slams it to his mouth, but it doesn't help. He gasps for breaths, head down. We all lean forward, trying to breathe with Willie.

"The inhaler's empty," Ms. Hill says.

Giovanni rushes out for water. Our teacher phones the nurse. Slowly, each of them taking an arm, Max and Gio walk Willie down to the nurse. We all lean into the aisles, watching them disappear. None of us can work. When Max returns, he says Willie's mom is rushing to school with a new inhaler. Willie forgot to bring it in after vacation.

After two whole days Willie shows up. He's breathing fine, but I keep an eye on him. Each week I ask him to shake his inhaler and make sure there's something inside. I never want to see him like that again.

It's cold enough to knit. My grandma's teaching me to knit a scarf, but so far all I've got is tons of holes. I plan on sending it to the homeless. Amber and Natalia want to learn, too, so I teach them how to do a knit row. Somehow we lose all the stitches and can't find them. Maybe they slipped underneath my desk. We cast on yarn and begin again. As her rows gain inches, I get the news from Natalia. She begged her mom to tell her everything about her birth mother. She's ready to hear the stories now. Here's hoping.

Then I hear Willie's news about his grandma. No, I didn't lean into the aisle or even try to eavesdrop. I'm sitting there innocently in my front-row seat when Willie tells our teacher. After that asthma attack, I knew something was up besides damp weather. That boy's getting so thin, you're gonna see through him soon. Willie's hurting and I gotta do something.

Ms. Hill, I'm bustin' here!

But if I say anything about it to anyone, she'll accuse me of gossiping (which I'm not).

"Can I make a suggestion?" I whisper across my desk to hers.

Ms. Hill's been writing reports on us. Her pencil keeps moving until she looks up and sees my face. I wear my serious eyes. Sometimes, I sense things nobody else knows. I know when something is up.

"I heard about Willie's grandma. And, wait!

Before you think the worst of me, I got a plan to make them both feel better."

Ms. Hill's pencil is stalled in midair, so I have a chance now.

"I really liked how you suggested that Willie write to his grandma. I've been watching him all day, and he's not getting to it. So, how about the whole class sending her a get-well card? I'll make one and pass it around for everyone to sign."

My teacher tries not to smile. She leans forward, across her big wooden desk, and whispers. "Go ahead. But you must ask Willie's permission first. You can't just step in and take over, even if it's a good thing you're doing—which it is!"

Willie's pencil is frozen on the page. Now's the time. But what if he doesn't like the idea? Maybe he'll hate it and me, too. After all, I am the class busybody. Everybody knows why I'm sitting up front—so I'll stay out of everyone's face. But if I don't make a move, Willie might stay stuck like that forever.

I walk over to his desk and say ahem. He looks up and studies my hair. I had it done for

Christmas and only now does he notice—fifty braids. Mine are shorter and springier than his spidery locks. Neither of us needs a comb anymore.

"Willie, I'm wondering if I could do something, if you thought it would be all right."

He looks through me like I was a cloud.

"Would you like the whole class to send your grandma a get-well card? It'll make her smile. She'll think she's famous."

His thin lips part. He doesn't say a word. Then I see the glistening in his eyes. He nods his head and looks away.

I dash to the closet for a piece of pink construction paper and make a huge card. Ms. Hill allows me to supervise sending it up and down the rows for kids to sign. We even sketch mango trees all over the card. The next day it's ready for mailing in a big manila envelope. Willie and I rush down to the office, where the secretaries promise to pay the extra postage.

"I wrote her, too," Willie says on the way back up. "With all those get-well wishes coming her way, she has to feel better."

That sure lit me up. Willie won't mind

whatever I say from now on. He trusts me. Don't I know what that boy needs? All you have to do is study people long enough to figure them out. Then they're not mysteries anymore. They're your friends.

FEBRUARY

"Writers aim their words
deep into the reader's
heart like arrows."
–Giovanni

ODE CRAZY

Maximo

Don't tell anybody, but I've got obsessions. I can't stop writing. That's not cool. Nobody knows about it yet, not even Ms. Hill. She buzzes around the class conferring with Tyrone, Petros, and Angel. Their notebooks have a few lines on each page. Petros doodles instead. Angel usually signs out for the bathroom during writing time. And Tyrone is Tyrone. He never pays attention. When she's through with them, all the ends of her hair stick up. By that time, the writing period is over. I like it like that.

Ever since that poetry lesson, I've been doing poems on the sneaky side. I mean in my head. On my way to school in the morning I even do it, instead of cursing how tired I am. In the middle of reading a book, an idea buzzes, like some annoying mosquito that won't fly off. Only if I give in and write the words down am I free.

Destiny's the poem queen. She struts around the room snapping her fingers, making up lines as she goes: *Poems are popping. / Words are hopping / in and out of my head.* Sometimes, she'll sing snatches of a song, passing through the aisles: *I never knew/ never knew/ someone as sweet/ as you.* When I see Destiny coming, I plug my thumbs in my ears. Once you hear that girl sing, you start singing, too. She's contagious! If you watch her during writing time, her whole right arm spins like she's scrambling eggs. She writes quick, in two breaths, then leans back in her chair and puffs out air. The next minute she's poking Chelsea or hissing across the aisle to Ah Kum. Like I say, Destiny is her own poem.

I can't believe I used to worry that I couldn't write. Poems visit me now and wake me up at night: *If they find him / what will happen? / Will he run/ again / or will he come back? / No way to know for sure./ It's a waiting game.*

I hunt for topics. Destiny tells me to write about the new people in my life or my friends. Excuse me, I don't have many, just Gio and Willie. Ms. Hill, too. My one and only Valentine Day's card came from her.

I will not write about Tom. He's getting to be a regular at our apartment. Phone calls, movies, and Godiva chocolate on Valentine's Day (I ate most of the box). He took Gio and me sledding during the February break. Bring a friend with you to the park, he said. I couldn't say no. I was dying for the slippery hills and couldn't wait all day for my mom to come home from work. Gio loved rolling downhill, his mouth full of snow. Hot cocoa and doughnuts at Dunkin' Donuts afterward. That night I fell asleep before my head hit the pillow.

I watched Gio and Tom, waiting for something to go wrong, like always. I'm the boy on the edge, remember? Well, Tom did not get tired of us. He never nudged us to go home like my mom would after our pants got soaked through and through. He zigzagged down the hill, screaming louder than us. But I will not write about him.

"I can't let all that stuff go on again," I told Gio afterward. "The problems my mom had with my dad."

"That stuff is over now," Gio said.

"Don't you get it? Tom will let her down. My mom will get hurt all over again."

"This guy is okay," Gio insisted. "Give him a chance."

Sometimes I think Gio knows nothing at all.

I am still stuck for topics. Then I find odes. They are like potato chips. Once you start writing them, you can't stop. You have to write more. An ode celebrates one thing. Way back when, in the old days, poets wrote odes about stupid stuff like love or urns from Greece. Yuck! We have them beat on weirdness. Amber reads aloud her "Ode to My Parrot." It begins:

How you squawk when you open your green eyes in the morning!

Then Jackson shares his poem.

Ode to a Potato
You live underground.
You grow invisible.
You sprout from tiny eyes on old potatoes.
You must see in the dark so
you are healthy to eat.
You love it when the rain falls on you.
You are ready to eat when fall comes.
You don't mind us digging you up at all.
You taste best mashed.

That does it. Our class goes ode crazy. Ode to a Prairie. Ode to a Quotient. Ode to a Desert. Ode to a Mayan Ruin. I wonder if I can ode about myself. That's a topic I really know. Why can't I write about me as if I was looking at myself from Gio's seat?

Here goes—

Ode to Maximo
He who hates celery.
He who likes diner food (when he can get it).
He who gets to stay up late when the Mets play
in the World Series.
He who cheers for the underdog.
He who never roasted marshmallows.

He who wears faded blue jeans every day.
He who disappears in a novel and forgets what
time it is.
He who remembers someone who never came
back.
He who wonders if he is remembered.
He who tiptoes on the edge—
Shall I trust? he asks.
He is the one who dreams somewhere
beneath his spiked hair.

When we trade drafts with our writing partners, I slip Willie my ode. He doesn't trade anything. We are supposed to write comments to our partner, tell them what we like, don't understand, or wanna know more about. Willie hands my notebook back with this note.

2/15

Most of this stuff I never knew about you. It was a surprise to me. Your last three lines make you sound mysterious. I remember trying to get to know you. It was tough. There's so much to know about someone. It takes a lifetime, I guess.

I don't get what people see in celery either. It's useless as a vegetable. I'm right there with the blue jeans, too. And, before I forget, can we go to the diner together sometime?

What more can you ask of a day but to fill it with odes?

NO PLACE LIKE HOME

Giovanni

Scuzi, Ms. Hill! Tell me, tell me what's next. Don't stop at the best part! I gotta know. I'm face-to-face with that deer and the wolves sliding past. WOW! The snow's all over me, and I shiver straight through. You can't shut this novel and begin the math lesson. I gotta know!

But there's just one copy of Gary Paulsen's *Woodsong* and Ms. Hill will only be reading a few selections from it. She says it's a book you can read in bites. We don't have time to read the whole thing. She doesn't even finish the chapter today. When she leaves it on a nearby desk, I grab it.

I slip the book wide open onto my lap and sneak peeks at it during the division lesson. The sentences come short and sharp. Then there's one sentence all by itself in a paragraph. My breath leaks out of me. For the first time, I know what writers do. They choose certain words. Each one is a feeling. Writers aim their words deep into the reader's heart like arrows. Mine is pierced through.

That afternoon I sneak the book home. Later, I read it underneath the covers with my dad's flashlight while my brother safely snores. I look for the lines that shine. Each sentence does. I read each line three times before I go on. That way, the words sink in deep. I am right there in the woods with Gary Paulsen. As I fall asleep, that scared deer presses in my mind. I see her jumping over the snow with nowhere to go. If I was there, it might have gone differently.

"*Ciao!*" I shout to Ms. Hill the next morning. "I know what happened!"

I tell her right away when she picks the class up in the auditorium. I can't wait until we get to our room.

She studies me closely, like the bug I thought I was.

"Gary Paulsen took us right into the woods

with him. He used all his senses. He made sure we wanted that deer to live, just like he did. But he also wants us to understand wild animals. We can't control them like pets."

My teacher's mouth falls wide open. She looks down at the book *Woodsong* in my hand.

"You took it home?" She blinks.

I nod. It's the first time I ever did such a thing, and she sure knows it. She doesn't even scold me for taking it without permission. When we get to 5E, she's got such a smile brightening her face, calling out good mornings to everyone.

If only I could tell her my dad was coming to Career Day, too, a special fifth-grade event in May. That would really give me extra points. She couldn't fail me then. Maybe she wouldn't write "HO" on next month's report card either. But he won't so I can't. He is too busy. I wonder whose parent will come that day. Willie, Destiny, and Max all say their moms have to work, too. Doesn't everybody's?

As we unpack our book bags that morning, Mrs. Rosenblatt's knuckles rap on the loudspeaker, waking everybody up with morning announcements. Soon her voice crackles loudly above our heads.

"Lice check tomorrow, children! No mousse. No gel. No hair spray. You must wash your hair tonight. Please remember!"

Nobody's listening. Asmir draws dirt bikes zooming over his math book. Mohammed scratches his head, so maybe he hears. Angel is hiding in the closet. Book bags fill the aisles. But the principal is not done. Her bracelets clink high notes against the loudspeaker, making us wince.

"Here's a special announcement. There will be a writing contest this spring. Any fifth grader can enter a poem, personal narrative, or essay. It is due on May 1. One winner will be picked and announced in late May."

Salute! It sounds like fun. I have loads of stories to pick from. I could even write more. Then I notice the shadow that could only be Mrs. Rivera. It quivers, all alone, in the back corner, ready to pounce on me. Bet she thinks I don't dare enter. Bet she believes I can't write just because I am on the hold-over list. I'm gonna surprise her. I'll get all my friends to enter with me. We'll form a tight huddle, like soccer players on the field, so she can't block our way. Maybe that will make her leave the room for good.

I check out Max. His head is down. What is he thinking about? Behind me, Willie sits absolutely still, staring out the window.

"Psst!" I bother Max. "What about the contest?" I whisper.

From across the row, Max frowns like he's got a mouthful of slugs.

"I can't write," he complains. "So, I'm not gonna enter it."

Who is he kidding? He can do anything.

"You're smart," I tell him. "And you can spell, too."

"That's not writing," he insists. "You write stories about Sicily, upstate, and your crazy brother. Real-life stuff like Ms. Hill wants. I've never done anything or gone anywhere. You always have ideas. I don't."

"Scuzi?" I say. "Here's something you can write about—sledding with Tom and me!"

That did it. Max asks me every single day what I think about Tom. So I finally told the truth. He's a nice guy. He hung out with us on his day off. My dad could never do that. He never has a day off. That snowy day I giggled nonstop. My laughs swallowed me up like waves diving right down to my belly. It was a holiday feeling.

Maximo throws up his hands. "I don't want to remember anything! I don't want to hear about Tom and how you think he's so great. He's . . . he's . . . not my dad!"

Max bolts out of his seat. The veins in his neck stand on end like his hair. The whole class stops working.

"YOU DON'T KNOW WHAT IT WAS LIKE!" he screams. "My dad hit my mom. He wouldn't let her be. I had to watch. It went on and on."

My chest spreads flat on my desk. I cover my head in my hands. When Max acts like that, it's best not to say anything. He hasn't been in one of those moods for months. Ms. Hill floats down the aisle and gently leads Max into the hallway. We follow them with our eyes.

"Lie to him," Willie warned me a few days ago.

"Don't tell Max nothin'," Destiny hinted with her head in the air.

I didn't listen.

I am afraid for Max. I want him to be my friend forever, and now I've blown it. He's got all those feelings inside, and they just burst loose. If only I hadn't opened my big mouth. What if he never speaks to me again?

But Willie and Destiny don't know everything. They weren't at the park with us. Max loved it. He laughed at Tom's jokes with me. Why won't he say so?

"Psst!" I hiss loudly across the room to Willie.

He turns around in slow motion. His hazel eyes are swirling.

"You gonna enter the contest?"

He stares right through me. It kind of makes me shiver. But he does nod. At least Willie and I will be in it together.

Max disappears for a whole period. Destiny says he's in the Guidance Office. I have never been in there, and never hope to either. They make you tell secrets down there. Max misses writing time. I don't write about what the rest of the kids are writing. Another topic finds me instead.

2/22

In the mornings, when it is still so dark, i think it must be the mittle of the night, i hear my dad stumbling around the kitchin. He tries to be quite but that's not easy with his size twelve feet. i won't see him until evening. We wait on dinner for him.

He walks in around 8 pm, plastered with flour. Little flecks sit on top his hair. He pats our heads with his big, smooth hands like we are balls of doe. He listens to my mom's stories about her day and smiles but it seems to hurt his face. He yawns nonstop, leaning back in his chair. Then he goes for a long soak in the tub. He's snoring by the time i head to bed with my novel.

sometimes, it feels like all i get of my dad is one cold slice of forgotten pizza in the box. A leftover slice.

When Max returns, he won't look at me. He's quiet. That's not like him. All of us are copying homework, just before dismissal bell. So I take a deep breath. It's worth a try.

"Why don't you come home with me tomorrow?" I ask him. "You'll see what goes on in my house, where nobody stops. Maybe you'll grab a story."

149

Maximo's pencil stops in midair. "You mean I can write about it?"

"You can borrow it. I've had enough of it, thanks."

"I'll ask my mom," he says.

And the way he looks at me makes up for everything. His lips lift just a little bit at the edges while the sadness still sits there, deep in his eyes.

The next afternoon it didn't take long at all for Max to understand what it's like to be me. He came over to my house and trailed my brother around with his notebook, trying to write a story about him. Mario wouldn't put up with it for long. He ran out the door when he heard his friend's motorcycle rumble past. Then we watched my sister blow-dry her hair, talk on the phone, and polish her toenails Hoedown Brown all at the same time. My aunt and my mother's cousins dropped by and never stopped yakking. Max had plenty of notes, but he couldn't figure out how it could be a story. He called it chaos, whatever that is (sounds like hot Mexican food).

After five platefuls of spaghetti and meat-balls disappeared in Max's stomach, his mom picked him up. I stood in the doorway waving good-bye, with the odor of spaghetti sauce and garlic brewing in the air and the voices of my aunt and mother laughing from the kitchen. My dad headed to his bath after patting Max's head good-bye and promising to let him roll some dough at Gloria's come Saturday. In that moment everything seemed perfect—Max walking into the quiet, and me heading back to the kitchen for my aunt's stories and another helping of spaghetti and meatballs.

STRETCHING STORIES

Willie

It's Friday night and we meet at the Greek diner on the boulevard—Max and Maria, his mom, with me and my mom, Katie. From the first moment the moms greet each other, they take in everything. Maria in her crumpled black sweater. My mom with roundness around her hips like she's packed volleyballs around her waist. Max with his hair straight up and his perky eyes that see straight through you. Me and my skinniness. More than half of me is hair, my aunts joke.

My mom settles right down into the booth making the cushions sigh. The two moms get to talking and forget about us. We are free to play with the ketchup, make jokes with the waiter, and fold napkins into paper airplanes.

"You and me both with these boys." My mom looks at Maria. "Sure is tiring. A big ache in me bones sometimes. But we are not stone broke, like back in Jamaica. We are doing fine now. No man to help us out either."

Max turns his head then. He loses that fresh look on his face. He stares at me like he never saw me before. I never said a word to Max about my dad. How could I? The mention of a dad would make him spit.

"It's been almost three years since we're on our own," Maria says. "I'm struggling to make ends meet. My paycheck can't be stretched further. We do without a lot."

"Be smart, *sistren*! Get your schooling done now. Study up good. Earn that nursing license. Double that nothing salary of yours in no time."

"That was my dream before I was married, Katie. But I didn't get to it. Never had the time or the money. Or a moment without worries."

My mom leans toward Maria and smiles. "One morning you'll wake like the sun, feeling bright, *sistren*. You'll fix everything right if you earn more money. Make your life sweeter. Gonna think about it?"

Maria nods. "I want a better life for Max. Sometimes he has a hard time believing it. Take the writing contest. He told me about it, but he won't enter it. He's taking to writing more this year, so I think he should try."

"Whaddup?" My mom sits up tall in the booth.

I sink down into the cushions while Max's mom explains it to her.

"*Me chil'* didn't say anything about this. We've been busy worrying on his grandma. She's home from the hospital now. My Willie helped her bounce back like a weed just with his letters. Those words he put down—that's good writing. I hope he's thinking about entering. Are you, *chil'*?"

I swallow. Across from me, Max is feeling like me. Trapped. He says he won't enter the contest but I want to.

Everyone is staring at me.

"Maybe," I mumble.

My mom gives me a sideways glance and raised eyebrows. She's a lot like Ms. Hill in that way. Can you tell me more about that? That's how my teacher would say it. Then our orders arrive and no one pays attention to us anymore. Max and I swallow our burgers whole. They are sky-high, salty, and hot.

Next day in the classroom, I get to thinking why I keep my thoughts inside and don't tell my mom. My grandma is the one I tell stuff to. I dream of being a writer. That's something I haven't told anyone because it just happened in fifth grade. My grandma loves to tell stories out loud, setting a hush on all the young ones. She's a William Shakespeare, my uncles say. That's what I want to do in my notebook. I like to write about Jamaica best. If I could tell it right, the sun would burst all over you when you read it.

I'm drifting when the fight breaks out between Max and Gio. Poor Gio. He stutters, red faced. Max spits his words out, the veins in his neck popping like steam pipes. We're all afraid for him. Later, when Ms. Hill sends Max down to the Guidance Office, a strange stillness settles in the room. We're stunned. Ah Kum bites her lips, eyes red. I've seen her dad. She drops her head down when she spots him after school. He starts barking orders soon as he sees her.

I can't help but think of my dad and how I didn't get to know him. Suddenly my breath becomes thinner. I practice the long, deep breaths my mother taught me, filling my belly first. Destiny swings her head around to see what's up. When my chest calms down, I grab my pencil, flip my notebook open, and let it out.

2/24

I was never mad at my dad. I couldn't understand anybody getting that mad until I heard Max's story. It wasn't fair. The only good part is that Max and his mom got away safe.

My dad didn't leave like that. He strayed all the time. When he finally walked off that day, my mom closed her heart. She decided to move to America.

She gave me a photo of my dad so I'd have something of him. He's tall and thin with a mess of hair. That part sounds like me. But his eyes make me shiver. Even then, they looked burned out like smoky ash when no fire is left. Sometimes I worry about him and sometimes I just feel sad.

I'd like to forget about him if I could. He's not coming back. If he did, there'd only be more sadness. I can't hope for it anymore.

But the wish slides in anyway, past all my thoughts, and wedges in my brain.

Where is he now and does he think of me?

Does he wonder how I look, what I'm like?

Does he ever want to see me again?

We all sit around in Writers' Circle one day. Everyone has trouble picking the right entry for the contest. I don't have that one perfect entry yet. Ms. Hill says we must develop one story or poem and stick to it now.

"Which story should we enter?" Amber looks puzzled. "Our notebooks are full."

"Can you tell me which one's my best?" Jackson begs our teacher, shoving his notebook wide open in her face.

"Reread your stories and look for one with promise," Ms. Hill answers. "One with feelings. Lines that shine. Review it to find places to open it up. That's what revision is."

She reads a few lines from a story in her own notebook:

I just met my friend's grandmother. She was very old and tiny. She sat in her wheelchair and waited for us to walk up to her. I really wanted to meet her.

Then she asks us, "What's the best line? One with details."

"How the grandma was old and tiny," Jackson says.

"What do you want to know more about?" she continues.

Ah Kum answers, "You never told us where you went to meet her."

"Yeah," Destiny adds. "Or who you were with?"

"Did the grandma like you?" Bo Wan wonders aloud.

"Great job!" Ms. Hill gasps. "Those are the questions I would want to know, too! Let me work on it for you."

Our teacher's pencil flies across the page. Jackson pops his head up to peek in her notebook. Destiny elbows him to settle down and wait. In a few minutes Ms. Hill reads to us again.

My friend and I went to a place on the boulevard to visit the grandmother of the family. She is ninety years old and can't walk anymore. In her wheelchair she looked very tiny and old. She wore a black dress because she lost her husband years ago. That is a tradition in Italian families. Her white hair was pulled back flat in a bun. When she saw me come in, her eyes widened. She asked me to come up close. She pressed my hand between her thin, cold fingers and wouldn't let go.

"Much better, Ms. Hill!" Jackson grins. "She really liked you."

"Who's your friend, Ms. Hill?" Destiny begs again.

Ms. Hill blushes. Her mouth drops open a tiny bit. The words are right there. We can all feel them, but they don't come out.

She sends us back to our desks to do our revisions. On the way I sneak peeks through Jackson's notebook. There's at least thirty poems inside marked with yellow stickies. So many to choose from. He captures a moment in time and freezes it onto the page. He's quick. I read over my writing entries. They are personal. Heavy. I could never share them, especially not in a contest. I wish I could be like Jackson. He hops around the room like a flea, snatching topics. He's in everybody's face. He doesn't wait for poems to walk by his desk like Maximo. Max is a watcher.

You have to be hyper to write poems. I move so slow, I don't even know there is a moment. And I can't write poems either.

GROUNDHOG DAY

Destiny

The groundhog pokes his head back up in early February and so do I. He says there's six more weeks until spring. Ms. Hill says I can go back to my regular seat. She lets me off for good behavior.

"You've done a real nice thing for Willie." She compliments me. "It gives me confidence that you're learning what to do with what you know."

Jackson's still up front, but I am back to my perch. I look around. This class is a bundle of nerves. Carmen kicks her sneakers at the desk legs and Dalma's hissing at her to stop. Natalia's awful quiet lately. There's Willie pacing and worrying and wearing out the tiles, waiting on word from his grandma. Does he think he's the only one? We're all waiting. We wrote her, too. We all have grandmas except for Max and Petros, and we know what can happen to them. They're fragile. Not one parent signed up for Career Day either. Ms. Hill looks disappointed every time she reminds us about it. Nobody's boss will let anyone off for a few hours just to visit a kid's classroom.

Then Max had that blowup.

We breathed a sigh of relief when our teacher finally sent him down to Guidance. Poor Gio. He turned pale as a piece of number 10 spaghetti. What I can't figure is why Gio is Max's friend. Is he just dumb? Can't he see what I'm seeing from my old seat? Max is bitter as a whole pack of sour lemon balls. Sometimes I want to grab Max's shoulders and give him a good shake. "GET OVER IT!" I'm dying to yell in his ear. But that's for his mom to do, not me. That much, I'm learning. That boy needs to be taken down a few notches to see straight.

Here's my prediction for spring. What's come into Max's life is bringing a change. He's going to have to change, too. My mom says Tom will make a good dad. Tom waited too long for the right one while he was busy going to school. Then he got too afraid to take a chance. When he met Max's mom, Maria, he realized that she missed out, too, just like him. They're a good pair, my mom says. The old ones at the nursing home call them sweethearts. I think they are brave. But I'm not saying a word about this to Max and certainly not Chelsea. Tell Chelsea, tell the world, because she'll tell her mom. I got my seat back and let's say I wanna keep it that way. I'm sticking to learning.

Here goes.

Ms. Hill says writers write about what's in front of them. The teacher is farther away now, but I check in regularly to see if she's still doodling. She is! Sometimes she doesn't notice our hands waving in the air. Sometimes we have to repeat our answers. She never did tell us more about her life, except that one grandma story. What is she thinking about?

What's in front of me now is all the different arm raises when the teacher asks questions. Jackson lifts his rear end off his seat and waves both arms like flags in a windstorm. Ms. Hill ignores him. My mom says our teacher is some kind of saint. Carmen's yawning. She has four siblings younger than her. She slumps in her seat, anchors her elbow to the desk, and waves a limp hand. But you should see Ramneet. He holds one baby finger straight up and eyes Ms. Hill like a target. She's always curious about what he'll say. Can you write a poem about hand raises? There's weirder topics than that, believe me, which leads me to my next observation.

Max's hair is flat. Then I remember. Today's a no-gel kind of day. The volunteer mothers appear at our door with a box of sticks. Pickup sticks, I call them. I can never work during lice check. I have to watch. One mother picks through Asmir's tight curls. His eyes roll up into the top of his head. He's afraid they'll find bugs like they did last year. Soon a stick wanders through my braids, picking them up and letting them fall. It tickles. I hold my hand over my mouth so I won't burst out laughing. Around me, girls remove clips, letting their hair loose. The smell of Ashley's shampoo drifts by, kind of like rainwater and spring flowers. It takes long minutes to lift up all her curls.

At Willie's desk two mothers stand on either side of him, flipping his dreads. He takes the record—ten full minutes for lice check. Best of all is Carmen. Her clothes never match and her black hair's usually squeezed into a tight braid. Her socks are always falling down. Sometimes she wears big sweaters on hot days. Today, her long hair wraps around her shoulders like a wild animal. She closes her eyes, mysteriously smiling.

Even Carmen's learning to knit. My grandma cast on stitches for her in this real ratty yarn of black-and-red stripes to match her socks. She keeps poking at the needles like they're chopsticks. Then she jabs herself. Ouch! Only Ah Kum knits perfect rows with those dainty fingers of hers. She has a real flair. Natalia is so busy telling me her secrets, she drops stitches like crazy. She found out her birth mom was very young when she had her, left school, and ran away. When her family found her, she did the one right thing. After she gave birth, she signed papers so Natalia's new family could adopt her right away. Every kid is their own story, I guess.

Poems pop up right around you. Today in

line, Dalma and Carmen suddenly screech.
They pinch and poke each other. I swear
someone's hair is gonna get ripped out. Carmen's face is purple mountain thunder and
Dalma flashes lightning from her eyes. Mr.
Miller's in charge of us at the time. We're on
our way to his room for computer class. He
makes them sit at opposite ends of his room
and not get a chance to use the computers.
That does it. Soon enough, they get mad at
him, not each other. And I, lucky girl, get my
poem.

Girl Fight
Suddenly
there's a loud scream
so high pitched, it hurts our ears.
That's how girls fight.
Pinch. Poke.
Hiss and yell.
Tears too.

By the next period, the storm is over.
They're side by side again
promising,
I'll be your friend forever, girlfriend.

Hug. Sway.
Dance and
Hop.
Girlfriends.

Near the end of the morning, I am busy whispering to Chelsea that Vinny the Hammer is visiting the Steinway Nursing Home every week now. My mom even saw him in person. He's wide and tanned with big muscles, and bleached blond hair. Vinny's the one somebody every boy and girl agree on—we are dying to meet him.

Suddenly the class buzzes. Whisperings all around me. Heads turn to the front of the room. Bo Wan gasps. A thin girl stands beside Ms. Hill. The girl's hair blazes bright with red highlights flashing on top of her black hair. It's the color of sugar-maple leaves, and it lights up the whole room. Against it, her face is wooden and pale, like a mask. I wonder if she's wearing makeup, which girls aren't allowed to do in this school.

Hey, I caught a moment. Finally! Let me just write it down real quick. Please, please don't interrupt me until I do.

MARCH

"You are all poems
in the making."
–Ms. Hill

COMPETITION

Maximo

It's freezing out. Boys sneak into blue-jean
jackets, shivering all the way to school, while
the girls still wear fleece hats and coats. Ms.
Hill announces the March ground is popping
and have we noticed? Just when it looks like
nothing's happening, she says, daffodils will
shoot up. We planted some in front of our
apartment building last fall on a patch of bald
ground everyone ignores, including the super.
My mom and I dug the bulbs in. Each and

every day since New Year's, I checked it out. Ten days ago, green stems finally poked up. The flower pods are growing slowly.

"They found your dad," my mom tells me one morning. "He's got a job in Florida. Part of his paycheck will go to our lawyer, then us. I'm going to nursing school like I always planned. No more double shifts for me. I'll study while you do homework."

All the times I asked. All the times I wondered: Florida. It has a name. Far off. Untouchable.

"He never said good-bye. Do you think he will now?"

My mom pauses. "Why don't you say good-bye to him first? That way, it'll be done."

"How can I do that?"

"Ms. Hill tells me you write about your feelings in your notebook. You can write a letter, too, like Willie did."

"But—we can't let him know where we are."

"Write the letter. That's the hard part. We'll figure out what to do with it later."

As soon as we step outside to walk to school,

we see one daffodil bursting in full bloom. I pull my notebook out of my book bag, borrow my mom's back, and write a poem on the spot.

daffodil

The color of soft butter in a dish
or a ripe lemon,
it stands
like a tall soldier
shivering
in the cool wind.
Blooming right there,
bright
in the dirt.

The poem rushes out so quick, I feel quivery inside. Before I can stop them, tears spring. I don't let my mom see. All this time I've been fuming at her. For leaving my dad. For moving around. For not signing up for Career Day. But those are the things she had to do. *The daffodil is her. She's the one who stood up all this time like a brave soldier shivering but still blooming bright. Why didn't I get it before?* I rush into her, my head down, and hug her a long time. Tom beat me to the first New Year's hug, but I got one now. The two of us kind of hang in the air, swinging back and forth. I don't ever remember doing that.

It never fails. Just when I get happy, everything changes that day at school. In walks a new girl with her dad, a bearded man carrying a briefcase. He looks important, like a principal or something. Imagine a dad taking time off from work to drop off his daughter.

Then I take a look at the girl. Superlong legs like a spider and a punky pink dress over her skinny body. She's got burgundy highlights on her poker-straight black hair. She's not a real redhead like Ashley. You know what skinny dyed-haired girls are like. They always want their way.

Behind me, Amber hisses the news.

"It was done in a hair studio. That's the only place to get such perfectly straight hair with highlights that glow like that."

"This is a new student. Please welcome her to 5E," says Ms. Hill. "Tell us about yourself, Tiffany."

All pencils clang down. The girls study her hair and clothes, all shades of pinks and reds. It's Tuesday, a gym day, damp as winter, and

169

they all wear jeans. The boys watch closely. We were chosen for 5E. We have been together since late September, like a family. Jackson once told us what it was like when his mother brought home a new baby sister from the hospital. Bet it felt just like this.

"I moved here from Florida," Tiffany announces. "My dad's an editor and got a new job in New York City."

Oh, oh! Bet her dad will be the only one showing up for Career Day.

"You may be surprised to hear what our class knows about editing," our teacher brags. "Can you tell her about it, Maximo?"

Tiffany's green eyes shift toward me like a cat's.

"We edit our work with our writing partner. Before Ms. Hill reads it, we must check everything."

"What kinds of things do you check?" Ms. Hill prompts me.

"Oh, spelling mostly." I grin at Gio. "Capitals. Periods. We see if the piece makes sense or if anything is missing. We add details."

Ms. Hill beams.

"My dad does all that and more." Tiffany

lifts her chin high. "He chooses which manu-script will be published. Only the best ones. And he knows famous authors, too."

I narrow my eyes. What is she saying—that we are nobody and only pretending to be writ-ers? Ms. Hill opens and closes her mouth, but nothing comes out. She assigns Tiffany a seat.

Everyone stares at the new girl heading down the aisle like she's tiptoeing on jewels. The only desk left is opposite Willie. He frowns. He's had that back corner all to himself. Each day he inspects the maple tree for buds. Now Tiffany's head will be in the way.

A thought slams like a spitball in my face— Tiffany will be in all our ways. She will enter the writing contest, too. Our class worked all year to become writers. This spoiled girl walks in and could grab the trophy from one of us. Gio really wants to enter the contest, although he's scared. I bet Jackson and Willie dream of winning, too. We all do—even Tae Hyun, who is just beginning to write sentences in English. It isn't fair that a fake redhead can come in and do this to us.

At lunch I squeeze between Gio and Willie, who are begging for extra fries from the lunch ladies. My buddies drop their jaws down making their faces long and skinny, pretending they are starving. Mrs. Lopez laughs and soon their trays are heaping. Ketchup packs spill out of their pockets.

"You know what this Tiffany is going to do, don't you?"

They drop their heads back and pop fries into their wide-open mouths.

"She's gonna enter the writing contest, and I bet she'll win," I tell them. "Her dad's an editor and he can help her."

Gio almost chokes. Willie gulps his fries down.

"Well, don't you wanna do something?" I bug them.

Gio shrugs. "What can we do about it?"

"Tell the teacher Tiffany can't enter the contest. We were here first. We worked hard to become writers."

"Ms. Hill won't like that!" Gio protests.

Willie blurts out, "You told your *main men* here that you didn't want to be in the contest!"

"Well . . . I don't! But I don't want her to enter either."

I storm off in a huff and sit with Mohammed. Perhaps he'll listen. But he'd rather arm wrestle instead. By the end of lunch period, I haven't found one boy who will come with me to see the teacher. Back in class, I raise my hand.

"Ms. Hill, I need to conference with you. Can I come up now?"

She nods her head, shifts her papers aside, and waits. Willie shakes his dreadlocks. Giovanni sits on his hands.

"Is it fair to let someone new enter the writing contest?" I ask Ms. Hill. "Someone who . . . didn't work as hard as we did learning to write. Someone whose . . . father knows more about writing than anyone."

"The contest is open to all fifth-grade students at PS 1. Are you in one of those classes?"

"Yes." I gulp.

"Is Tiffany in fifth grade, too?"

"Yes."

"Then she can enter."

"But—her dad will help her and she'll win!"

Ms. Hill flips through her plan book with her Candy Baby nails.

"Maximo, I am curious. Will you enter the contest?"

I am burning up. I stretch the neck of my T-shirt open to let air in.

"I don't know yet."

"I hope you do."

My big conference is over. All I can do is sink into my seat. Social studies comes and goes like a breeze passing through the room.

"Boys and girls, here's a reminder about the contest," Ms. Hill says. All heads turn her way. "Each of you must do your own work. Write entries in your notebook first. Include all drafts to show how you worked on them."

Over Tiffany's pale skin, a bright flush creeps. She strokes her notebook. It has brass binders and a pink plastic cover. It doesn't look like our notebooks, more like a diary. Willie passes me a note with the news:

Miss *Hightey-Tightey*'s fancy notebook has only a few short stories inside.

It's just the news I want to hear. The red-streaked girl missed all of Ms. Hill's super writing lessons. Our notebooks are chock-full. Jackson and Ah Kum already filled one notebook and started second ones. I heard Ashley carries her notebook home each night and fills it with dreams and poems. Even Willie is filling his notebook, too, although nobody knows what's in it.

This new girl thinks she can beat us. No way I'll let that happen!

STORY IN THE OVEN

Giovanni

That afternoon, sliding down the railing on the back stairway after school, Max finally talks. Since lunch, his lips were zipped tight as saran wrap.

"If we can't get rid of her," Maximo decides, "we'll join her!"

"*Scuzi?*" I ask.

"We'll beat Tiffany at her own game."

"*Wha???*" Willie's mouth hangs wide open. "I'm not highlighting these dreads!"

"No! No! No! What I mean is . . . between the three of us, one person has to come up with a winning piece of writing. Three against one."

"But—you told us you weren't going to enter the contest!"

I wait at the bottom of the stairs. Now my mouth is hanging open like a garage door.

Max shrugs. "I changed my mind."

"Did you forget about the rest of our class?" Willie reminds him. "They're gonna try for the writing contest, too."

"Yeah," I argue. "Jackson and Destiny pop up with some good stuff out of nowhere."

"Don't you guys get it? It's okay if someone else in 5E, 5A, 5B, 5D, or even 5C wins. As long as it's not her."

Then Max holds his palm flat out. "I'm in. Who's gonna join me?"

My palm slams against his.

Then *wham!* Willie's hand bangs ours. *"Yes, mon!"*

All that night my thoughts spin like bright marbles. If I don't do something now to change my life, I'll lose Max and Willie. Next year, I'll be stuck in fifth grade with Carmen's sister. I heard she drops spitballs on your seat behind your back as you sit down. If I could win this contest, it'd change everything. Mrs. Rosenblatt wouldn't hold me over. I'd be famous.

But the next day Ms. Hill hands out spring report cards. Amber, Max, Bo Wan, and Ashley flash 4s in reading. With my 1, I don't pass. That's the worst mark you can get. Everyone's smarter than me. Even Lin gets a 2 for effort because he strings some words together now. I press my thumb over the hold-over box so no one will see it. Mrs. Rivera still hangs over my head like a rain cloud.

I keep thinking about that conversation I had with Willie. It plays over and over in my mind like a CD on replay.

3/12

"Mrs. Rivera wasn't mean at all," Willie swears. "Just worried."

"About what?"

"About us. We were her job. She was hired to make us smarter. The mayor won't pay teachers if our scores don't go up. He thretaned to fire them. That's why she watched us carefuly and sat so close."

I had to sit down. I couldn't even open my mouth.

If this was true, Mrs. Rivera sure lost money on me. I'd been with her two hole years and showed no signs of progress. Poor Mrs. Rivera. She must have been starving on her celery. No wonder she wore the same dress every whensday and had those circles beeneeth her eyes. Mario had it all wrong. She just wanted me to learn, especialy after failing with him.

What can I do to win? Max says we need a game plan.

"Let's meet outside after lunch," he whispers to Willie and me. "Bring your notebooks with you."

Willie nods.

I haven't a clue where to begin. I flip through my notebook. I can't believe I wrote so many entries. Observations. Stories. Thoughts. Wonderings. It's a collection.

The morning drags. Somewhere between science and current events, Ms. Hill's voice fades in and out of my ears.

". . . revise a piece of writing . . ."

I kick a dust ball to see if I can make a goal between Max's sneakers. *Whoosh!* It slides right through. *Salute!*

That's when I hear cooking directions.

"Once you choose and read your entry, put it aside a few days. Don't peek! I call that 'sticking it in the oven to bake,'" our teacher says.

Max's head swivels to the front of the room where Ms. Hill stands. But nobody seems interested. Tyrone bends paper clips into shapes. Amber and Chelsea are mouthing silently to each other. Ashley twirls her curls around her fingers. Tiffany's nose is stuck in her book. Her hair glows like parrot feathers. It hurts my eyes to look at it.

"You should notice something to change," our teacher continues. "Something you didn't see before—like a misspelled word. Read it aloud to your partner. Add a detail. Or a short, snappy title. Something to make your writing stronger."

Willie's eyes land right on mine. They have a secret light in them. Ms. Hill just gave us the recipe for the winning entry and nobody listened but us. We both check out Max. He gives us the thumb, straight up. He motions to us to take our notebooks when we go to lunch. I can hardly wait for the noon bell. The three of us will slip our notebooks beneath our jackets, wiggle our pencils behind our ears, and whistle out the door. We'll be ahead of everyone.

Grazie, Ms. Hill!

BORN TO WRITE

Willie

3/19

My grandma still doesn't write back. But I pump out the letters to her anyway and drop them in the mailbox. When my aunts come over, we call long distance to Jamaica, our ears flattened to the receiver, my mom hushing my young cousins. My grandma's voice cracks when she hears us. Her breath is raspy. I picture her sitting down in the rocker in her living room with a view of blue sky and sea. She thanks me for my letters and I can feel her smile even across the distance.

"All fruits ripe!" she says. "I'm back in *me* house, eyes on the sea, *easing up.* Don't worry now, Willie."

But I do. I lost someone before.

In our kitchen is a calendar where my mom marks our schedule: work days, school holidays, and the plane trip to Jamaica on the day after school ends. I count the time: three and a half whole months to go. What if I don't get there in time? What if everything slips away from me again?

I'm waiting for things to change. And they do. It becomes spring. You know what happens in spring? Thunder and lightning. Sudden storms, too. My *main men* and I are sprawling on the blacktop in the playground after lunch one afternoon. It feels warm from the sun. Gio, Max, and I confer about our stories with our writer's notebooks wide-open when the girls sweep past us, like a dark rain cloud, Destiny in the lead.

When I'm with Max, I have to be like him and bad-mouth girls. I'd never tell him how easy it is to look at Destiny.

"Here comes Miss *Labba-mout,*" I announce to Gio and Max. "With all the *sistren.*"

"*Che cosa?*" Gio smiles.

"Chatterbox!" I interpret. "With her girlfriends."

They both crack up as the girls stop in front of us.

Dalma's hair is blow-dried flat and so is Carmen's. I don't think she ever combed her hair before. It looks like someone sat on their heads overnight. Chelsea keeps smoothing her hair so everyone notices the five superblonde highlighted streaks in her black hair. The four girls hang out, elbows leaning on one another's shoulders.

Destiny shouts in our ears. "I'm a front-row girl so I sure heard you bad-mouthing Tiffany with the teacher, to get her out of the writing contest!"

"You boys are just jealous 'cause she's a girl," Carmen yells. "And her dad's some-body!"

Gio slips behind Max like his shadow will protect him. I give the girls my big nasty look.

But Max does not budge. He stares right back at the girls without blinking. "Tiffany never learned to write from Ms. Hill like we did. She doesn't belong in 5E or in any con-test."

"So what?" Dalma shoots right back. "She learned to write from her dad!"

Max folds his arms across his chest. "She does not have a chance. None of the kids in the other classes are gonna win this contest either."

"How do you know?" Destiny stretches her neck out like a rooster about to crow. "You a fortune-teller or something?"

Giovanni swallows hard. It's a boy-girl fight and a good thing his girlfriend Ashley is nowhere in sight or he'd be dead meat.

Max sneers at the girls. "You wanna know how I know?"

The girls face Max, standing still. Kids gather around, expecting war. In the playground all the shouts die down. Even the wind stops.

Finally Max speaks in a voice so low, we have to lean in to hear him.

"If we had stayed in the other teachers' classes, we wouldn't be writing like this. Whatever Ms. Hill does, rubs off on us. I would not be a writer, except for her. You either. One of us should win."

He flips open his writer's notebook. Page after page is filled with stories and poems. No doodles. Just words. Kids gasp. Destiny narrows her eyes and straightens up. Something falls out of her pocket. It's a ball of yarn. She picks it up. Carmen, Dalma, and Chelsea all flip their flattened hair back. The 5E girls don't say one word. They turn and walk away in a tight huddle.

Max laughs. "That sure took the wind out of them!"

Gio grins at Max like he's a hero or something. But I groan. All I can think is now that Max opened his own *labba-mout,* one of us three had better win. Every fifth grader in the playground heard him boast. They'll all try to compete against us just to prove Max wrong.

Then something pushes up from my heart to my throat. It's not an asthma attack. It's a poem! A first!

My dad's long gone—
he's the past.
He will not be back.

Our stories are for now—
for telling how it is.
They're our future.

They will come
again and again
if we let them.

Soon as I finish writing it down, I give my two *main men* an order.

"Quit celebrating! Let's get down to work!"

The three of us sit in a circle, reading our work aloud. That's our game plan to pick our best piece. We'll use every trick Ms. Hill taught us to make the whole story shine, not just one line. We'll edit it without any help from our moms, who wouldn't know how to do it anyway. The teacher did say we can help one another. Cooperative learning it's called. That's where you borrow someone else's brain because yours isn't big enough. We figure it'll increase our chance at winning. We need the odds. *Yes, mon!*

GIRL BONDING

Destiny

I knew those boys were up to something. They're afraid of competition, namely that Florida girl. They're jealous because they think she must have an interesting life and loads to write about (they don't). Who wouldn't want to live in Florida and wake up to sunshine every day? The boys have her all wrong. Sure she has attitude. So does Max. Tiffany glows with that artificial hair and is lean as a rap star. I think she has charisma.

"She'll have beauty tips to share." Amber hopes.

"There's money there," says Carmen. "Her dad's a big shot."

"She could take us shopping and give us some hints," Dalma adds.

I'm the first to go up to her and flash my teeth. "How you doin', Tiff!"

I slam my palm down on her shoulder. It feels like a stick. She's thinner than Ah Kum. She's all bones. Perhaps she doesn't eat. Maybe that's why she's so pale.

Tiffany stutters a hello. She looks up at me like I'm a big tree plunked down in the middle of the classroom. I know I'm tall with big feet and a motor mouth to go with it, but I am friendly. Do I have bad breath or something? I have a plan. I decide to watch her closely. No big scoops until we get to the lunchroom. There she arranges all her food in size order on the table: carrots, ham, cheddar cheese, and bread. By the end of lunch period, she takes one mouse-size bite of cheese, that's all.

That night, at the dinner table, I question my mom.

"What do you call it when a girl doesn't wanna eat?"

My dad roars. "What girl? Anyone around here?"

He points to my plate, heaped high with three servings of honey sweet potatoes (my favorite), two hamburgers with melted cheese, whole wheat bread, and green beans. I elbow him.

"You mean girls who get so thin they get sick?" my mom asks.

I nod. "Why do they do that?"

"I saw them at the hospital on my first job. Anorexics. They were almost invisible. Poor things. They couldn't enjoy anything. They wanted to be perfect. Starving themselves was the way they thought to do it."

"What did their families say?"

"Their parents were sad. But they needed to look at their kids and pay attention to them. Try—"

My grandma cut in. "Give 'em lots of love, so they know it."

"And sweet potatoes!" My dad laughed.

I keep it a secret. I don't even tell my mom.

After all, Tiffany is keeping it a secret. I'm on her side no matter what she does. I'll defend her against that pit bull Max. Ms. Hill notices things, too. I know she studies us. Only she keeps it quiet.

"How do you know just what to teach us?" I beg Ms. Hill one day. "Do you read our minds or something?"

"I watch you kids. You show me what's next. If Gio gets stuck on an ending, I teach the whole class to make a circle. Go back to read the beginning and make sure your ending matches. You need the same lessons."

"Why did you become a teacher?" Ah Kum stares at her.

Ms. Hill sighs. She plops in her chair. It's almost the end of the afternoon, and she's been reading our stories and conferring with ten kids on how to improve their work. She can't do it anymore.

"When I was young, I was so excited about writing. I always got A$^+$. I even won a national contest and had a poem published."

We smile. But our teacher isn't smiling back. Her eyes mist.

"But I stopped. And all that promise, that joy, vanished."

What happened to Ms. Hill? We watch her silently. When she finally looks up, Natalia's deep-well eyes are fixed on her.

"My mother died and everything changed. I didn't write anymore—until I became a teacher. Then I started writing again. I may have lost my mom, but I gained a new family teaching kids. When you lose one thing, you find another."

Natalia swallows hard. I slip my arm around her neck and hang there. The girls huddle by Ms. Hill's desk. Chelsea and Amber move in close.

"When I see kids like you, I see that same promise. I know there's a lot out there pulling you down, just like there was for me. But I believe you'll get through it. You are all poems in the making."

"We promise we'll win the writing contest!" I tell her. "We don't care if it's a boy or a girl, but one of us in 5E is gonna win for you."

The teacher hugs us good-bye that day. Each of us gets a turn. Even Tiffany. She looks stiff as a pretzel ready to snap. I can tell she's not used to anyone holding her. Not me. I jump up and down and scream for joy. None of the boys come up, though. Gio stares at us with his mouth dropped to his knees. Boys don't understand girl bonding.

Hey! I am no longer on the outs with Ms. Hill. She hugged me!

APRIL

"I want to find the poem
hiding in the moment."
–Maximo

FINDING THE POEM

Maximo

The rush is on. I am not ready. I flip through
my notebook but can't pick a story for the contest. *I am waiting.* All my entries are too private. When Ms. Hill gave me thumbs-up to
write about my feelings, that's all I did. I folded
the pages in half like she suggested when we
don't want anyone else to read them. *I am
waiting.* My notebook looks like an accordion.

Ms. Hill shares selections from *Childtimes,*
a real old book written by Eloise Greenfield
with her mother and grandmother. They look

back through the generations of their family, snipping little snapshots out of their lives to share. Memoirs are hot right now, Ms. Hill told us. Authors make a lot of money giving away their secrets. It's not a sad book like the teacher usually reads to us. But it ripples through me with sadness all the same.

I never had a "childtime;" I would like to, though. I want to find the poem hiding in the moment like Ms. Greenfield does. Her book is about family, brothers and sisters too many to count, while I am on my own. My memories are shadows I want to block out: the shelter, hand-me-downs from church charities, hiding in the temporary house halfway to nowhere. I wish I could sit in my own grandmother's kitchen like the author Cynthia Rylant. No wonder these authors can write. Their grandmothers' stories fill them up like fresh baked bread.

4/5

I am waiting for something. Waiting.

Each day I run down to the mailbox to peek inside. Checks arrive from the lawyer's now. It's what my mom wanted. She enrolled in nursing school. I hear her asking Tom strange questions about cholesterol and heart blockages. It must be helping because on all her tests so far, she gets A's. But there's no letter from Florida addressed to me. Willie says he writes his grandma every week, but she is too sick to answer him. He writes anyway.

Sometimes when I walk past the old apartments on the avenue, I stop to watch. If it's warm, all the families are outside barbecuing, with loud laughter and music. My mind shoots right back to the nights when I lay awake in that building. I hear echoes of that long ago time. Crying. The arguments. My father's face is blurry, unsmiling. He walked away. He walked too far. That's why I'm not there with the barbecues.

I do not want to remember things about my childtime. It never happened like in the books.

Gio has a childtime. So does Willie, even without a dad.

I am stuck in neutral, waiting for mine to begin.

I break my pencil tip. This is way too personal. Why can't I write something normal about myself? Mostly I lie around reading.

When I read, I disappear. I'm not me any-more. *Can you say more about that thought?* That's what Ms. Hill would say. She'd grab it for a topic, so why don't I?

Where a Reader Goes
I stretch out
far as forever
reading on the couch,
disappearing inside the pages.
Becoming . . .
A survivor. An artist's apprentice. A kid with a
dog.
A brand new me.
I could live anyplace at all.
Reading
my way somewhere.

When it's 2 P.M. Tuesdays or Thursdays, it's writing partner time. Willie and I get to hop out of our seats and sit knee to knee on the rug. I read my poem aloud. Willie says my poem has a dynamite title. But he doesn't say how to work on it. That worries me. Ms. Hill says we can't see our own mistakes. They must be like dust mites: tiny, but multiplying all over the page. We need an audience, another pair of eyes and ears to notice them.

Next I show him my memory of last summer with the barbecues. Hope it's not too personal. In a memoir I think you can get away with that.

Willie looks into the air. "Ms. Hill says I gotta start off with a compliment, so . . . I love that word *echoes.*"

Then Willie pauses so long I get nervous.

"What's the bad news?"

He shrugs. "Not much happens, *mon.* Some yelling. Barbecues. Walking around."

"How about adding another fight or two?"

Willie shakes his head. "It's all about feelings. I want to know more."

I sigh. He's beginning to sound a lot like Ms. Hill.

"That's IT!" Willie shouts, making all the writing partners turn their heads. "It's not a story. IT IS A POEM!"

He underlines words that go together, each phrase as long as his breath. He puts *echoes* by itself. I get the shivers when I see what he's up to. Back at my desk, I rework it. Willie's right. It's a poem.

Home
Sometimes I remember
arguments
echoes
words as loud as slaps
each and every night
my mother crying long into the dark
then a silence so loud it startles the air
I don't hear it anymore.

But summer nights when
all the dads, moms, grandpas, and kids sit on the
stoops
with the windows open and stereos blaring
and the steaks are frying on the barbecue
I wonder
where those letters are
the ones I have been on hold for

Short lines give my poem a bare-bones feeling, like the brown winter tree outside our classroom window. Each day the tree reminds us about the way it used to be, full of buds and maple leaves and birds singing. It remembers what it once had. The white space around my poem is the ache, the absence of a dad.

I may not be able to write about a childtime or a grandmother, but I sure know about losing somebody. It leaves a dark space inside. All you want is to close it up, don't dare look at it. But it keeps peeking out at you, catching you off guard. When you wake up from a nightmare in the middle of the night. When you watch Gio's dad in constant motion yet checking out Gio with his eyes. When you see Tom trying his best to make you laugh, not giving up on you, the way your own dad did.

Last night I finally asked my mom why my dad couldn't be a dad.

"Why did he change when I was born?"

She sighed. "The problem came out when you were born. But it was there all along. Your dad couldn't handle money or bills or jobs. He had all the wrong friends. The truth is your dad couldn't handle anything. And I just made excuses for him. I was to blame, too."

"What!?"

"I waited too long for him to grow up. That last visit to the emergency room, I looked at you. Really looked. It woke me up. You were so small and yet so angry. I didn't want you to grow up like that. It gave me courage to leave."

I got goose bumps right away, big ones, shivering up and down my back. It wasn't me! I wasn't the one to make them split up. I want to stop looking at what went wrong all the time. I'm not saying there's not pain. There is. But there's sparks of joy, too. Both of them live in me, side by side. Maybe they could be friends now, like Willie and me.

Dear Ex-Dad,

    The last time I saw you, you didn't say goodbye. Neither did we. I wonder if you knew it was going to be forever. I didn't. You never tried to find us either. I wonder how long you thought you could go on hurting my mother? I am sorry. Sorry that I wasn't the one to stop you. She did. It's only now that I'm in fifth grade (on my way to sixth) that I can see what a great mom I have.

    You could have been a great dad, too, if you tried. Dads don't have to be perfect. They just have to be there. Take time to bring you somewhere you are dying to go. Maybe they try to make you laugh when all you do is pout. Or they like you nearby even though they are busy. Just so they can keep an eye on you. It sounds easy doesn't it? Maybe there was no one to teach you how to get along with people the way I'm learning now.

I just wanted to tell you that I'm growing up without you. I never thought I would.

Good-bye,
Max

TWO FOR ONE

Giovanni

"Two heads are better than one."

That's what Ms. Hill says when it's writing partner time. I bolt down the aisle to meet Ashley on the rug, spilling my books on the floor. Since Ashley's been working with me, I don't have to sit with the teacher anymore. The teacher drops in our conversation, nods, and moves on. Ashley's the one who saw the writer in me.

"You watch everyone." Ashley grins at me. "You notice every little detail. Why don't you write your observations down?"

Well, most stuff I can't tell anyone. Like the breeze when Mrs. Rivera flies by. She sat above my head during the whole citywide reading test. All I did was sweat. But now I think it wasn't Mrs. Rivera after all. Maybe it was my own worries. What if I lose Ashley? She won't ever talk to me again if I stay behind in fifth grade. She'll grow up without me.

Maybe she'll like my list poems. You just make a list, like you are marking down groceries. No big deal. Lists aren't big on punctuation. You don't even have to write sentences. You can whip them up quick as peanut butter sandwiches.

I wrote two list poems about being outside. Most of the winter, we are locked up in the auditorium like in jail. We dream of bursting free into the fresh air. By the end of the school day, especially Tuesdays when we leave at 3:30, the sun is sinking behind the tall buildings. A bitter sting cuts the air. We all crave the sun like candy.

Ashley leans forward to hear my poem. Her hair spills over her sweater like golden threads. It's hard to keep my eyes on my notebook.

Spring Is . . .
sunshine
after days and days of gray

outdoor lunch
puddles and red cheeks
the first time you sweat
wind in your hair
the world wakes up
and so do you.

Ashley's cheeks turn pink from all the fresh air blowing in my poem.

"That's it, Gio! Didn't I tell you to write down the stuff you see? We all feel alive when spring comes."

I read her another poem.

The Playground
Flying in circles
clockwise and counterclockwise.
Fifth graders. First graders.
Hopscotch and leapfrog.
Double-Dutch ropes spinning.
A hundred balls rolling.
Running with eyes closed like bats.

Ashley closes her eyes while I read. When I'm done, she pops them open. "I can see it, Gio! Everyone's moving like crazy in the yard.

It's a miracle nobody gets hurt. But why did you write about bats?"

"'Cause they can't see. They follow sonar waves or something."

"What a good detail. Can you add that to your poem?"

"Yes . . . but . . . which poem do I enter in the contest?"

She shrugs. "I think you should do something strange."

Scuzi? She leans closer to me. Maybe she'll whisper, "I like you!"

"Take details from each poem. Like kids making circles, jump ropes spinning, and the bats. Then you'll have one great poem."

I usually get a lot out of writing partner time with Ashley. Mostly, I study which curl is winding into another one and where it ends up in all the twisted vines of her hair. But today, Ashley gives me the greatest idea. Goose bumps pop up on the back of my neck. I can't wait to try it.

Spring in the Playground
Wind and sunshine
after months and months of gray

they let us free
for outdoor lunch
it's the first time you sweat
hopscotch and leapfrog
double-Dutch ropes spinning

We fly in circles
splashing through mud puddles
fifth graders clockwise
first graders counterclockwise
eyes closed
like bats
following sonar waves

This is the poem I will enter. Today's the deadline for deciding, and I have zoomed to the finish line in time. *Grazie,* Ashley!

Across the room Ms. Hill is setting up a projector and screen. She says she'll hook it up to a computer to teach us word processing and editing. We'll be ready to type and edit our entries after that.

Suddenly, our teacher rushes from the computer to the phone.

"Oh no! The computer monitors are on a trip! They can't help me!"

Ms. Hill's hair frizzles up like it's a summer day. My bleached blonde aunt says sometimes ladies can turn gray right on the spot. I study Ms. Hill to see if there's any sign of it now. Not yet. She's still brown-headed.

Mohammed soars out of his seat like a rocket. We only see him move like that in gym. He fiddles with some wires leading out of the computer, yanks the wall plug out, then sticks it back in again. Suddenly the projector brightens and hums.

"Way to go, Mohammed!" Our teacher finally smiles. "5E—we're hooked up! Your work will look so professional, the principal will have a hard time picking the winner!"

She opens up Microsoft Word and begins a new document. Somewhere in there are folders for each of us to store our work, she says. My fingers roll on my desk to this crazy beat. Asmir hisses at me to stop but I can't. I want to hop right up and type into the projector screen.

"Save! Save! Save all your work as you type! When you're done, pull down the spell-check from the Tools menu to check for mistakes."

"Can we print it out, then?" Willie wonders aloud.

"No. Let your writing partner edit it first. Save the changes. Then print."

"How do we edit onscreen?" Ms. Hill asks us. We all shrug.

The teacher types a sentence. No period. No capitals. Weird spelling mistakes, too. She swears it looks like writing she's seen around. Our hands wave in the air like wings, attacking errors like hawks. Ms. Hill stops the little blinking cursor to the right of the mistakes. Letter by letter, it gobbles up the word backward! If only our writer's notebooks had such magic.

Mohammed shows the class where to find the spell-check and print commands from the menu. The printer cranks up and spits out paper. It's hot! It's fresh off the press!

"Tomorrow," Ms. Hill announces, "the monitors will bring in the cart and we'll type our entries. Is everyone ready with their work?"

"Yes!!!!" we all shout.

All around the classroom, we chatter noisily about the cart. Petros says he's seen it pushed around the school. It's fifteen laptops all charged up and ready to go. It rolls on wheels, and it's coming to 5E tomorrow. How am I gonna sleep?

Computer Crazy
Gimme the keyboard please!
My fingers itch for it.
They are hot to trot all over that mousepad.
Give me the smooth feel
of the keys beneath my fingertips.
Little finger. Index finger.
Pounding out the words.
Give it to me now. i gotta have it.
i wanna drive my words
straight onto the screen.
Zoom!!!

CUT AND PASTE

Willie

This class is high voltage. It feels like a hurricane's ready to blow in. All eyes are fixed on Ms. Hill. No one whispers. Angel does not doodle. Gio does not play soccer with his footsies. No one even turns their head when the phone rings. We all wait on Ms. Hill to give us a word about how to polish our stories.

But I am still stuck on what story to enter. My writing is all about the same thing. So I mail five entries off to my grandma and beg her to pick the best one. She's gotta answer me now. She'll know I'm in trouble. I need her words and in a hurry, too. Forget Career Day. Stories are up first.

That was four weeks ago. Each and every day, I check the mailbox in the lobby. No thin airmail letters wait inside. Just bills. Advertisements. Announcements of Easter sales.

The night before the deadline, a thin airmail letter sticks out of the mailbox.

Dear Willie,

You know I like the one about why Jamaica's so special, don't you, *chil'*? This story sweeter than the rest. Lots of love inside. Love of a place. Love of family. Love of a mango tree.

You sure know how to put your words down. You make me see this place like I was looking at it through sunshine. It's always been *irie* to me. Here, *me* grandson come to feel the exact way I do about *me* homeplace. How did you know that the one thing to get me moving out of that hospital and on the mend was *me* own mango tree?

Don't worry about all the long days ahead to summer. Just remember that no matter what...

school boun fi gi recess!

Do you know my meaning, Willie? It means that sooner or later, school will have a break! School will end in June. So, even if it's cloudy now, the sun's gonna come out later. Just wait for it.

WALK GOOD!

Grandma

P.S. See you on June 29!

Please thank that *chil'* Destiny, the one who wrote so big on the get-well card. She must be a dazzling girl. Tell her I feel her *irie* wishes shining across all these miles.

I jump so high I thought I'd touch the ceiling. My grandma's getting better, I just know it. She sent me a sign—a letter! I have the best writing partner of all, and she's a secret. I don't even tell Max. He's been waiting for me to show my story to him. Today is the day.

Squeak! Squeak! All heads turn. The silver

cart rolls down the hallway. It stops in our doorway, grinding to a halt.

Voices call out. "Stop here! This is 5E!"

In comes the rolling cart pushed by two computer boys, monitors from sixth grade.

The wheels creak, "We're here! We're here!"

"Check it deep!" I call out to my classmates.

Destiny screeches. Angel dances in the aisle. The whole class turns *chatty-chatty*. Kids jump up out of their seats and head to the cart. We don't want to wait to get our fingers on the keyboard. Then Jackson, who's been perching on his seat like he's gonna take off, finally falls off his chair. Ms. Hill gives us the look. We all quiet down to listen to directions.

We begin by playing musical chairs. Max slides into Mohammed's desk next to me as Mohammed rushes off to join Tae Hyun. Max nudges me when Amber squeezes between Destiny and Ah Kum. Amber's partner, Tiffany, is absent today of all days.

"Miss *Hightey-Tightey*'s not here!" I elbow Max.

Max grins like a cat with a fat mouse in his paws. Our rival is sick while we sit with a shiny new toy on our desks. Everything is thumbs-up.

I start to type. Max peers down at the story in my notebook and complains it's clumped together like peanut butter. It needs paragraphs, he says. I didn't have a moment to fix it.

One of the monitors sneers as he walks past. "How come you didn't edit your story yet? We don't have that kind of time, kid."

"You sure keep your writing a mystery." Max sneaks a sideways look at me.

I point to his notebook, with each page folded in half so nobody in the world can read it.

"So do you."

Max shrugs and reads my story, word for word. But he doesn't give his opinion. I always tell him what I like about his stories. I even convinced him to choose between "Home" and "Ode to Max" as entries for the contest. He picked the ode finally. Max is silent now. The only time he does that is when he's reading Gary Paulsen. It makes me nervous. My story must stink and Max is too loyal to tell me and my grandma is too kind.

Suddenly the screen highlights one of my

words. Something in my brain lights up, too. I'm writing about my grandma and Max doesn't have one. That's why his face looks flat as if my words ran over him.

But it's just the word *duppy* that's all lit up.

Max leans into the screen. "What does that word mean?"

"*Duppy,* like you know, stories we tell at night in Jamaica. The kind that give you goose bumps."

"Ghost stories?" Max's head jerks my way.

I nod. "Should I change it?"

Max drags down the Tools menu. The dictionary gives us strange choices: "dupe. dude. dumbo." It's none of those.

"They don't know Jamaican." Max grins. "Ignore it. Keep typing."

I key like a mean machine. *Tap! Tap! Tap!* The letters jump onto the screen and line up, run straight across, then head to the next line all by themselves. Max points to where I should begin new paragraphs. My words look more important on the screen than they ever did in my notebook. Definite. It seems like a real story now.

"Check this." Max points to a line onscreen. "This part about the sunset could be moved down. You should describe mangoes, too. Not everyone knows about them. And tell how you feel hearing *duppy* stories."

I read it through. My heartbeat quickens. Max is right. Why didn't I see it before? It's sticking out as big as Asmir's foot in the aisle. I add some details, but when it comes to moving lines around, I freeze. What am I gonna do now? My time is almost up and soon it'll be Max's turn to type.

"Psst!" Max calls the other computer boy over.

He's one of those cool sixth graders, with straight blond hair tied back in a ponytail and jeans riding so low, off his skinny hips, they might fall down at any moment.

"I wonder if you could help my friend." Max points to me. "He doesn't want to type his whole story over, but he'd really love to move some lines up. I bet you're the only one here who knows how."

The boy peers down at us like he's some guru high up on a mountaintop. I kick Max's foot. That's what I'd like to do to this monitor, too, but, instead, I stretch my lips into a wide smile.

Then, so quick I can't tell what he does, he zings his fingers over the track pad, highlights my sentences, and presses something. ZIP! In a flash all my sentences totally vanish. I rise up out of my seat. My whole life of ten years flashes before my eyes. I can't breathe. My story is *gaan*! Then that blond boy leans over and presses another command.

In a flash my sentences fly back from outer space where they've been floating homeless, and they land right back down in the spot I prayed they would. *Yes, mon!*

"Thanks!" Max calls out to the back of the monitor's sweatshirt.

"Whaddup?" I plop back down in my seat.

Max laughs and pulls down Cut from the Edit menu. He shows me how the monitor dragged his finger over the track pad to highlight the words, then pulled down Paste to stick them in the exact spot I wanted.

My mind is twirling with those sentences that were just flying out there in the netherworld. You can make words disappear and come back again and the words will land down smooth.

My story is DONE! I am BEYOND *irie*!

TRUE CONFESSIONS

Destiny

This Max itches me like a mosquito bite. He's organizing those dreamers of boys he hangs with to win the writing contest. They cluck over those entries of theirs like a flock of hens on a nest of eggs. Girls write much better than boys. None of us liked seeing all of Max's work, though. We thought for sure he was just doodling in that notebook, but he wasn't. He was crafting stories. Go figure.

I watch Max all morning. Then I see my chance. As he gets up for lunch lineup, a piece of loose-leaf paper floats off his desk down to the floor. It's the entry he's been working on so furiously, his head close to the page, his pencil clocking in at forty miles per hour. This is the one, I thought, the prize entry he is submitting to the contest! Just let me get a sneak preview. I wait until everyone lines up. I'm in the back since we go everywhere in size order like a set of chess pieces. Chelsea does her bit. She distracts everyone at the front of the room by elbowing Tyrone. He shouts at her. Soon Ms. Hill quiets everyone down. That's when I snatch up that paper in my hot little fingers.

I don't pull it out of my pocket at the lunch table, although my friends are all whispering for me to. I have to be discreet. Besides, I have become Tiffany's life coach. Not that she hired me. But, I am coaxing her to eat. She sits across from Ah Kum and me. I spread out my whole lunch in front of Tiffany and ooh and ahh over it. She keeps checking it out. First, she tried a sweet potato fry, and then the next day, chewed some slices of pot roast. One day she took a bite of Ah Kum's bean cake and asked for more. Then she ate all my turkey and stuffing, so I had to eat her lunch—lasagna stiff as rubber with a sauce so sour, it made my mouth pucker. Probably frozen food. Then I hit the root of the problem. Her dad can't cook. No wonder she won't eat. Maybe knitting will relax her.

I wait as long as I can without peeking at Max's paper. When we are seated in the auditorium for part two of indoor lunch, I open it. I lean back, my grin wide, ready for my scoop.

But it's not an entry. It's a letter addressed to "Ex-Dad." All at once my fingers shake. I know I shouldn't read it, but my eyes are glued to the page. I read it once and have to read it again. I snap the letter shut and shove it deep into my pocket. I can't look at anybody. A deep hurt bangs my heart. It's like I'm inside Max looking at the world through his eyes at the dad who walked off with no good-bye.

This is not the Max I know. This is a boy who's been trying to learn that no matter how hurt you are, you can still go on. Even if your dad never loved you and your mom. He didn't know how. All your dad knew to do was to push you away. No wonder all Max wants to do is fight. That's all he knew. I've been fighting Max, too. Here's a boy who's more grown up than me. I couldn't take the kind of pain he's had.

Up and down my row, I hear the hissings. The calls to hand over Max's paper. Chelsea, Dalma, and Carmen all stretch their hands out to grab it. Ah Kum's eyes catch mine. Her face darkens. She sits very still, like a rosebud jammed shut. She begins to shush the others.

"Shhh! He'll hear you! Leave Destiny be. She'll tell you later."

When everyone sits back, I finally let my breath go. I am chilled to the bone. All shivery. I should not be caught with this piece of paper. It's private. I looked into Max's heart without permission. I am a sneak. Go on and say it. My dad would. In my mind I see the shock on Ms. Hill's face if she ever finds out. She trusts me now. I remember the wincing look she had when Max threw that fit about his dad. And how she always lingers at his desk each day to check how he is. How am I ever gonna return this without anyone knowing? Why did I do it? For fun. For mischief. I always have to know everything. It would stun Max if he knew.

I hang with Ah Kum in the hallway on the way back to class, leaning on her narrow shoulder. I am about ready to cry. I tell her everything—how I make a mess of everything, how even my knitting looks so holey and lopsided, not even a homeless person would wear it, and how I'm afraid Willie might just stop talking to me altogether.

Ah Kum sticks her bottom lip out as she listens, staring at the other girls. Everyone wants a piece of the letter. All the girls wait on us.

"Slip it into my pocket," she whispers.

As she brushes past me, I stick it into her back pocket. If there's anyone I trust, it's her. I don't trust myself anymore. Or those girls. Giving gossip to them is like feeding a pack of starving seagulls. After the first crumb, they swoop back for more.

Inside the classroom I head straight to my seat. As usual, all the boys fight for the bathroom pass. Ah Kum slides in between them so they have to step back. Max is in front. He dives for the pass first. The boys all complain as he rushes out the door. We head to our seats. Our teacher does not allow lingering. Ah Kum walks the long way around, to the back of the room, past Max's desk. She bends down to pull up her socks and gently drops the letter on Max's desk. Nobody saw, just me.

I don't deserve a friend like Ah Kum. She keeps secrets. I don't. I'm gonna have to learn to keep them now. Then I remember how she's got her secrets, too, and I've guessed most of them. I never told her, though. I never asked. I never pried like I do with all the rest. Maybe it's her way of thanking me.

That afternoon I look way across the room at Max. He sits up, alert, his back in a straight line, not his usual slouch. He looks like he's got everything in order. He's a boy with a past, with an edge. He may always have that. How can you just let go of what's been dumped on you? He's braver than me. I could not live without my dad's teasing and his arms around me. Without my sister Lakeisha's saucy looks. Or my mom explaining the whole wide world to me. Max had to learn how.

He's not a pit bull after all. He's just solitary, a boy of secrets. He's like one of those mysterious blue herons who fly alone in a world of their own. Why was I ever against him?

Song for Max
I had you wrong.
You were hurting all along.
I never saw,
never saw
your tears before.

If friends had wings
I'd fly right over
next to you
and sing and sing—
I had you wrong.

MAY

"We never guessed. We never knew. We are the promises. We are the poems."
–Destiny

MY NEW BEST FRIEND

Maximo

The rolling cart stays for five days. We type and type, but some of our stories vanish into thin air. Willie says they go to the netherworld (wherever that is). They are gone for sure. Most of us forgot to save. But not Willie and me. We are into advanced stuff like cut and paste, centering, bold lettering, and cool New York font. The blond computer monitor likes to brag so he shows us all his tricks.

Willie has some story. I kept pushing him with the paragraphs. Otherwise, I would have to cry. It was that real. I sure would like to meet his grandma. I never met anyone who likes to eat outside like that.

Finally Tiffany shows up, her nose tomato red from a spring cold and her highlights dimmed down. She still hasn't signed her dad up for Career Day. She sets her typed entry on Ms. Hill's desk. The teacher reads it over and nods, patting Tiffany's shoulder like she's congratulating her for handing it in late. She never did that with us. She doesn't hand it back to Tiffany either. It doesn't need correcting.

"Know why?" I sneer in Gio's ear. "Probably her dad typed it. He wrote it too."

"Leave her alone, Max," Gio says.

I stare at him. Something has seriously happened to his brain since he and Ashley became writing partners. Willie says Ashley put an *obeah* on him—some kind of spell or something.

Finally, twenty-two entries on gleaming white paper are sent down to the office with Asmir, inside a folder titled, "WRITING CONTEST: 5E." Even Tyrone, Petros, and Angel handed in entries. I thought I'd hop up and dance when the stories left, but that's when the worries started up, like big army boots kicking around in my stomach.

Maybe I should have entered "Daffodil" instead of my ode. No one would guess it was really about my mom. What am I gonna do with that letter I wrote to my dad? I didn't show it to anyone yet. And just how are we going to sit still and wait for a couple of weeks until Mrs. Rosenblatt decides who the winner is?

Gio doesn't mention the contest much. Instead he obsesses about getting his ear pierced and wants to know what we think about him highlighting his jet black hair with blond. "Will it look like skunk streaks?" he wonders.

I'm losing my best friend to a girl.

The other fifth graders whisper in little groups around the playground, eyeing me. I never should have opened my mouth to brag about 5E. What if none of us win? Willie's eyes burn whenever the kids mention it. He worked so hard on his stories, keeping them secret. He incubated them like eggs, kept them warm, watched them grow. Even Destiny's acting strange. She lowers her voice around me and kind of tiptoes. She keeps telling me what a great writer I am. I don't get it.

On the third Monday in May, the loud-speaker crackles. Mrs. Rosenblatt's bracelets click in our ears.

"Attention fifth graders! We have the results of the writing contest!"

Amber slaps Destiny to be quiet. Mohammed sits straight up. All over the room, kids freeze their bodies like mime artists. On the way to grabbing the bathroom pass or rummaging through desks, hands and feet stall in midair. Ms. Hill plops down in her chair, pulling her long hair up as if she's hot, although all the windows are wide open.

"The writing entries are OUTSTANDING this year! It was difficult to decide on a winner. The committee decided that there can't be one winner."

Gio holds his breath. My stomach does a fluttery flip.

"So," the principal continues, "we picked one winner and one runner-up!"

"WHO ARE THEY?" Destiny yells at the loudspeaker.

Tap! Tap! Tap! "The runner-up is . . . Tiffany from 5E!"

Tiffany sits still as a park bench while all

the girls cheer. The boys look over at me. I feel like someone yanked my tongue out. Class 5E's chance to win was snapped away by Tiffany, like I predicted.

Tap! Tap! Tap! "PLEASE quiet down!" The principal orders like she can hear us. "We have a first-place winner! It's Willie from 5E for a heartwarming story."

We burst out of our seats. The girls twirl one another around. Ms. Hill cannot shush us up. How can she? She's the first to leap out of her chair to hug Tiffany. Then she heads straight to Willie for a handshake, but she can barely make it through the aisles. I dive over the desks and fall on top of Willie with a bear hug. He throws back his head and laughs, his dreadlocks whirling. Up and down the aisles, kids dance and throw their no. 2 pencils high up in the air like confetti.

"It's like an Italian wedding!" Gio shouts.

Willie yells, "It's a *bashment*!"

None of us notice when they slip into our classroom. Ms. Hill flicks the lights on and off five times before any of us look her way. There, in front of the class, flashing the winning entries, is the committee who selected them: Mrs. Rosenblatt; my second-grade teacher, Miss Chu; and Mrs. Giambruno. They wait as we all head back to our seats.

"We are so excited that such good writing is happening here," says Mrs. Rosenblatt. "Every single entry in this classroom was outstanding."

The principal points to us, setting all her bracelets clinking a song. "I remember how in September some of you were not happy to leave your teachers for 5E. Look what an opportunity you had to learn writing. It would never have happened without Ms. Hill and such a small class. We have the parents to thank for that."

Everyone claps. I give her the thumbs-up, and she smiles back at me for the first time ever. She hands out prizes to Tiffany and Willie. We all stretch our heads up to see: $50.00 gift certificates to Barnes and Noble plus July tickets to the Heavyweight Boxing Championship. Cool!

"Let's hear the winning entries. We'll ask Tiffany to read first."

Tiffany turns a strange color. Kind of like a

persimmon. She shakes her head at the principal, making her highlights shimmer in the sunlight.

"I would like the boys and girls to know what it is like to be a new student. Tiffany learned so much from being in 5E. Can you read your essay aloud, Tiffany?" Mrs. Rosenblatt hands the prize paper to her.

Tiffany swallows hard. She nods her head to finally say yes. But as she reads aloud she trembles like a little leaf on a winter tree.

At Home

Back home in Florida, my grandparents and parents spoiled me. I was the only girl in the family. I got whatever I asked for. But, no matter what new outfit or hairstyle I had, it never made me happy. It only lasted the first time I wore something new. They tried to make up for what I didn't have, I guess.

My mom and dad fought a lot. I felt like a piece on a chessboard, pushed back and forth between them. A pawn. All through the divorce, my grandparents hovered, my mom pushed, and my dad yanked. Afterward, they all let go. My dad got custody and a new job in New York. My grandparents stayed behind. I won't see my mom until August when she's out of rehab. I don't know yet how she'll be.

I did not guess what I really wanted until I came to PS 1. Class 5E was like a real family. They listened to one another and helped each other become writers. My dad never has time to do that. His work is more important than life I think.

Everyone belonged in a group when I came here: Max, Giovanni and Willie; Destiny and Ah Kum; Carmen and Dalma. I didn't. It took me a while before I realized the problem was me. I was on the outside. A girl without friends. No one even wrote to me after I left Florida. Now I know why. I was the best dressed girl with her head up in the air. I wanted to look perfect. That way, no one would guess anything was wrong.

But here, I had another chance to make friends. I began to listen to the other kids instead of bragging about myself. I changed into sneakers and jeans, like the other girls. I asked for their advice on my stories. I even ate their lunches.

Things began to change. My secrets began to drop like little pebbles in my trail. I hoped someone would pick them up and find me. And they did.

These girls saw through all my fancy layers. I wanted what they had. Not to be different or special. Just a fifth grader.

Home is the place you find yourself at. It's where you make friends with whoever is there beside you.

Silence fills the classroom. One by one, our heads turn toward Tiffany. Ms. Hill starts clapping. The girls join in first and then all the boys. We smack our hands like crazy. Tiffany is still this strange color. The principal shakes her hand and then Willie's hand. He slides down in his seat. His story will be read aloud next.

Suddenly, Tiffany bolts out of her seat and signs out, grabbing the bathroom pass. I am dying for ice-cold water, so I sign out, too. My mouth is sucking the water fountain and getting only a trickle of droplets warm as spit when Tiffany walks past. The hallway is empty except for us two.

"Hey, did you really mean all that?" I ask her.

It feels weird because I never actually spoke to her before.

She nods. Her head is bent down so I can see her dark roots. Having your story read like that in class must be like running naked down the hallway. None of us would do that.

"Did you write it with your dad?"

Tiffany looks up. Her blue eyes are not clear. "My dad doesn't know I wrote it. I would never show him my work. He'd ruin it with red pencil. I never wrote anything until I came to 5E. He . . . doesn't have time for me. He won't even take off for Career Day."

Her chest heaves. I know I gotta say something to stop her from crying.

"Congratulations! Our class has two winners. We are the best writers."

I stick my hand out for an old-fashioned handshake. You can't high-five a fancy girl. Tiffany bites her lips and tries to smile. It's the first time I ever saw her do it. Her face doesn't look so skinny anymore. In fact, up close, even her cheeks look rounder. She touches my hand lightly as if her fingers are feathers. Right then and there I know her story is the truth.

Hey, I want to say, *you belong in 5E, same as me.*

I think I was a little too friendly to her, though, because the next week, someone phones my place. My mom makes a big *O* with her lips when she answers, then hands me the receiver. "Tiffany!" she mouths silently. By the end of the phone call, my mom's grin is stretching to places it'd never been before. But I'm frowning. Ever get called by a girl who hangs on every word you say? It's a big job, let me tell you.

I have more important things to do.

That week, I hold two letters in my hand for the post office. I show the first one to my mom.

"I did it," I tell her. "I wrote to him. Now what?"

"Can I read it?" she asks.

The letter was already sealed. It was between my dad and me.

"Well, if you really want to mail it, Max, you can. We'll send it through our lawyer. But, then, you may wait all over again for him to answer. That might not happen."

She walks closer. "I can't bear to see you waiting for your life to begin. You don't have to send it. You let your feelings out. That's the important part, not whether he responds or not. You could just rip it up."

Rip it up? After all that! My mom doesn't

know yet, but my life has begun. I have to run or I'll be late for pizza rolling with Gio's dad.

I hand her the letter. "Send it to him. I'll mail this other one myself."

My mom leans over and sees the second letter addressed to Tom.

She smiles. "Oh, it's sealed, too. May I ask what's inside?"

"An invitation." I grin. "To Career Day."

Thoughts pound in my head as I head down the avenue. I yank my notebook out of my book bag. I'm learning to write on the run.

Hey, Mister Postman
A letter goes where we cannot go,
way out beyond us
traveling
into the future
where it will reach someone
and make them think of you
and wonder
whether they write back or not.

I always run late getting to school each morning. I show up at 8:19 A.M. and rush inside when the bell rings. Tiffany waits for me now outside the school with her dad. She's like a spider sitting in a web. I have to pass by her to get in the door. She gushes at me like some waterfall, saying she wants to measure my neck for a scarf. Her dad thinks it's funny. So does Gio. He laughs every time I look his way.

"*Scuzi,* Max!" he whispers. "Better get your hair straightened. My sister can do it with an iron and an ironing board—real cheap!"

Sometimes in the school yard, Destiny and Ah Kum walk past me, arm in arm with Tiffany of all people. Destiny winks as she goes by like she knows some big secret of mine. But, the worst thing is Amber teasing me. She calls Tiffany "my new best friend." She bugs me about how I need some highlights to match Tiffany's. She says she could do it for free with a bottle of bleach and red food coloring. Yuck!

FRESH AIR

Giovanni

There's big changes in 5E. A new woman keeps haunting our room. It's the principal! Day after day, she comes by. She even invites other teachers from our school to watch us write. They walk around and read over our shoulders. They are studying us so they can teach other kids how to write better. They're jotting down notes about us, too. All the teachers stand straight and stiff even though they usually seem tired. Mrs. Nelson peers over her glasses and Mrs. McGonigle's there, too, yanking at her collar in the sudden May heat. Destiny says she's gonna retire in June.

Ms. Hill glows. She walks from desk to desk to show the principal all our stories like she's our parent. The principal seems like our grandmother because she keeps smiling so wide.

That very week, my mom decides to visit Ms. Hill, too. She wants to check how I'm doing since the last parent-teacher conference. When she signed the spring report card, she felt she condemned me. The threat of the holdover never went away. It was like a big black germ. My mom wanted to hear the awful truth about my repeating the grade before I get my final report card.

Scuzi, I'm a new boy! I want to tell my mom. Even though I didn't win the contest, I entered it. Ashley loved my poem. I go to the library on Saturdays now. Max, his mom, and

I even spent a whole afternoon at Barnes and Noble bookstore last weekend. Max and I sprawled out on their nubby beige carpet. Believe me, it was a lot cleaner than the one in our classroom that's unraveling thread by thread. We leafed through all the books. Brand-new books feel smooth and cool, kind of slippery. They have a clean smell.

My mom even catches me sneaking batteries and then finds the flashlight beneath my pillow. I'm reading, I tell her. She sees the books from the library but doesn't trust that I am actually reading them. Hey, I don't get every word but I get enough to go on.

Is that reading? I wonder.

Reading isn't just words on a page like I thought. It's the things that begin to happen in your head. How the words explode, so fire-bright, you feel like jumping up and screaming, "I get it!" You begin to guess what the author really wanted to tell you.

But my mom comes to school anyway. At all parent-teacher conferences, my mom drags my aunt or me with her, because she never understands what the teachers tell her. All she knows is that I need help, but she's not sure what kind. As my mom and I wait for Ms. Hill, my face is in my new book like I was Max. My mom has to drag me inside.

Ms. Hill says something I will never forget.

"Giovanni hears and speaks another language at home. Italian is in his head. It's a big switch for him to read novels in English. That's confusing. Reading is harder for him than most kids. But he will catch up. I see progress. He's reading on his own. That's a big step."

You know how I felt? Ever go to swat a bug and suddenly notice how different it is? Maybe it's got fluorescent yellow stripes like no bug you ever saw before. You just can't swat it! Instead, you study it carefully awhile, then let it go. That's just what my teacher does to me. She will not hold me over. She sets me free.

Grazie, Ms. Hill!

Then finally it's Career Day. As soon as Ms. Hill picks us up that morning, there's a stir in the auditorium. The girls turn their heads and buzz like a zillion bees.

"Look!" Chelsea screams. "Ms. Hill's wearing a ring!"

So the teacher's got a big, fat, sparkling

ring. I shrug. So does Max. Willie yawns. He's not awake yet.

Destiny gives me the elbow right in my ribs. "Her left hand, Gio. Ring finger. Diamond. As in engagement. We're talking marriage here."

Girls sure rush into things. They discuss the teacher endlessly. But Ms. Hill won't talk. She laughs when Destiny stretches her face in hers and begs her, "Please tell us who!" Our teacher waves all their questions away.

I have my own worries.

I had kept my sister a secret from the class. I never mentioned her, although I said plenty about Mario. What if only my family thought her work was the best? But Ashley gave me away. She knit a scarf full of holes like Jarlsburg cheese. Her rows were crooked, too. Even I could do better. So I brought it home. Anna Marie tore it apart and redid it in an hour. Ashley beamed when she saw it and wouldn't stop gushing about my sister. I had to invite her today or Destiny was gonna twist my arm.

When Anna Marie appears at the door, Destiny zooms right over to her. She must be learning my family's history going back ten

Sicilian generations because they yak a long time. My sister stands in front of the room while we listen to her talk about how she designed her outfit. It's crisp black linen sewn into a strapless dress for a prom. All the girls look her up and down. They ooh and ah. Ms. Hill jokes that she'd like my sister to take an order for a wedding dress. When Anna Marie shows her best knitted sweaters, the girls bust out of their seats to feel them. They gather around for a knitting demonstration.

Max's eyes roll. Willie is still yawning. That's when Vinny the Hammer shows up. He must have heard the party from outside the building or something. All six feet of him fills the doorway, his bulging muscles touching each side. Ms. Hill rushes over and invites him in.

"Class, this is my friend Vinny. Please welcome him."

Heads turn. Our teacher actually slips her arm through his.

"Is he the one who gave you the ring?" Destiny blurts out.

Vinny laughs. "You didn't tell them yet? Kids, we're engaged!"

At first, silence stops everyone. We all stare at Vinny, who grins real wide, and at our teacher blushing beside him. One of the most famous people we will ever know is going to marry our teacher. She'll be famous, too. Jackson lets loose and jumps up in the air. Destiny and Chelsea smack hands and even Mohammed does a little dance. The girls hold our teacher's wrist up to the light and ooh and aah over the shiny ring. The boys line up by Vinny for autographs. We take them on our writer's notebooks, our bare arms, even on our T-shirts.

Just when I was wishing that my dad would come and make everything perfect, I see Fabio at the door. He's the deliveryman at Gloria's. He walks in carrying six extra-large boxes of pizza. The boys surround him like moths. Max and I stretch our slices way far away from our mouths to show off the cheese. My dad found a way to make it to Career Day after all.

All the girls are knitting wool Anna Marie gives them, so they don't rush over. Except Tiffany. She grabs four hot slices for her and Destiny. Boy those two can eat.

"Tiffany's a *wanga gut*!" Willie laughs.

Then Tom arrives from work in a blue scrub

suit with a stethoscope swinging around his neck. He steals the show with his doctor jokes. He says he wants to make sure we're alive so we get to listen to our own heartbeats thump. It's hard to get near him. Destiny's at one elbow, blinking her eyelashes like crazy, and Max stands by his other elbow.

5/29 Noticing Max

You should have seen Max. He was lit up, like a firefly. Not complaining as usual. Or scowling. Destiny's eyes were popping out of her head. She didn't recognize Max. Neither did I.

Max never took his eyes off Tom. He even tried to stretch himself high on the tippy toes of his sneakers to look as tall as Tom. He helped quite down each kid before Tom set the stethoscoop to their chest. He shushed the other kids leaning around while that boy or girl listened to their hearts all muffled with their mouths dropping open. He made sure everyone got a turn.

He and Tom moved like partners, the way I'd seen my dad and brother do at Gloria's, my brother rolling doe, and my dad sprinkling the toppings over it. Each one thinking the same thoughts. A little thread connecting the two of them. Side by side.

At the end of Career Day, I am finally ready for my big moment in fifth grade. It's something I planned after the last parent-teacher conference. I beg the teacher for fresh air, fanning my autographed T-shirt in my face like a flag. Willie lowers a window with one swift touch of the window pole. I whisper a good-bye prayer to Mrs. Rivera swirling up in the air somewhere. Nobody's gonna listen to her anymore. Not me. Or Ms. Hill. I close my eyes and take a deep breath. The air smells fresh, like upstate. You don't ever get that in this neighborhood. That's how I know Mrs. Rivera is gone for good. I sure hope she gets a job someplace else. She needs the money.

Addio, Mrs. Rivera!

KIDWRITER

Willie

Kids ask me about Jamaica all the time. Everyone thinks I'm an expert. They are all dying to visit there. For now, they are Destiny's customers. She braids strands of kids' hair at lunchtime. She brings bright beads like they sell on the beach and tucks them into your braids if you trade her candy. She'll do mine free of charge, but, *mon,* I'm keeping these dreads.

One night I looked through my shell collection. From a shoe box, I took out the starfish. It had swept up onto the beach one morning. I had tried to soak it with seawater and bring it back to life, but it never moved again. When it dried perfectly, I took it to New York. I wrap it up in tissue paper and hand it to Ms. Hill one morning.

When she unwraps it, there's such a surprised look on her face. She strokes the starfish with her Candy Baby nails.

"Why, Willie, it's so beautiful. It feels rough as sand. I can imagine the blue sea it swept out of. You have taken such care, too, to carry it all the way here from Jamaica to show me."

"It's yours." I close my lips tight.

She looks up with turquoise eyes that are like the sea. "This will always remind me of you and your stories. Thank you."

I turn away as the girls gather around Ms. Hill. Behind me, I hear them gasp and gush out girl noises. Ah Kum begs to touch the starfish. "Please! Please!" she squeaks. Everyone giggles. Tiffany says it belongs in a special place, just for memories. She'll bring a shoe box tomorrow and line it with felt from our storage closet. The girls promise to bring in little things to always remind our teacher about us and our stories.

Then I hear something I shouldn't. Girl stuff. Natalia spilling out her secrets in the sunlight and smiling about it. She shares the things her adoptive mother saved for when she was ready—a photo of her birth mother at fifteen, a Christmas portrait of her first family, even a sketch of the flat Texas lands where Natalia was born.

I read over my winning entry again. It surprises me how it spilled out. Writers should write what they know about, Ms. Hill always says.

Crosses to Lay Down

There's a place in the world where you can learn to let your troubles free. You have to look hard to find it. It may be far away like it is for me. But it will feel like home the instant you see it. Soon I will fly like a seabird across all the miles until I see the turquoise waters of Jamaica, then rise up above the hills, and land in the white house with the pillars where my grandma waits.

There's beauty in that place and magic too. It's in a mango tree. My grandma said that one tree taught her there must be sweetness in the whole world. You can't eat her mango chutney, or bite into a juicy orange slice of a *fit* mango without a smile brushing your lips, and spreading down to your belly. *All fruits ripe,* my grandma believes. This means that all is good.

Perhaps this feeling comes from being outside so much, surrounded by family. We make a circle, sitting around, my grandma at the center of everything. Outside, where the sun bakes her herbs dry, is where my grandma says her kitchen is. That's where my aunts, my mother, all my cousins and I like to eat evenings, underneath the wide arms of that tree because it makes the thickest, darkest shade to hide you from the setting sun. We don't go back inside the house until the sun is long down and the stars hang icy in the sky. Little shivers creep up my bare legs by then from sitting in the sand all evening listening to my grandma tell stories of the old times. Skeletons and magic are always in them. *Duppy* stories, we call them.

When the moon is high, I finally go inside, flop

down on my cot, where the sound of the sea fills my ears as if I still swim in it. My body rides up and down with the waves. When the day ends, just as you are floating to sleep, you know you have done it. Your *crosses* are no longer part of you. All your troubles have dropped down into the churning waters and disappeared. You can forget everything there, like my grandma once promised me.

I never feel alone in Jamaica, even at night, when the rain taps on the tin roof of my grandma's house like it's telling stories. It fills all my holes.

There's so much I want to say. It heaves inside me, swelling like waves rolling one after the other. I'm bits and pieces of everyone. Part of me is still with a dad who wanders the streets. Part of me hovers over my mom, who is not home when I awaken in the morning but gone early on the subway to her shift at the hospital. The biggest part of me roams over the sea, by the bungalow with the tin roof where my grandma sits on the porch, listening to the rain story-tapping above her head.

I was never all in one place before. I always drifted in my head. I can visit home anytime now. It's right here in my writer's notebook.

Wherever I go, I carry it with me. It'll ride in my backpack on the plane to Jamaica with all my new books from Barnes and Noble. I won't dare take a chance and check it in with my luggage. I'm almost packed. Just a few weeks to takeoff.

Writing is like taking a long walk out to a place where nobody else is. Far from everywhere. No one's there to tell you if you are right or wrong. Something invisible as wind pushes your pencil across the page. Before you know it, you've stepped into the country where stories come from. I think you're there when words fly from your mind to your pencil tip without your even thinking. You look up when it's over. The room does not seem the same. It's brighter, sharper, like you are looking at it through a magnifying glass.

A boy and his notebook are *cook and curry, mon*!

HERO WORSHIP

Destiny

I don't know if this is an end or a new beginning, but here goes.

There's so many heroes in my school life: Max, Willie, Tom, Ah Kum, Ms. Hill, and Vinny the Hammer. Let me get to the headline news right away. I'd only seen Vinny in posters on telephone poles and in the windows of Italian delis. Never in person. Up close, he's a bronze god! Like the ones you read about in myths. I can picture him riding his chariot to victory. Beside Ah Kum, he was a mountain man. Salon-tanned skin, Chelsea said, with oiled muscles. He's a man with curves. Now I know what Ms. Hill's been daydreaming about. Who could blame her? I know you are wondering how the news got by me. A girl can't know everything.

The most handsome hero of all is Tom. Those old folks at the Steinway Nursing Home were right. He's an eyeful. A real hunk. There's something sunny about him. Max sure needs that. He gave a great performance on Career Day.

"Let me give a listen," Tom said when Gio couldn't find his own heartbeat.

Tom got all serious, leaning over Gio and listening hard. He shook his head, frowning. He couldn't find any heartbeat either. You should have seen Gio's face. His mouth dropped down to his knees.

All of a sudden, Tom patted Gio's head and smiled.

"Got it! You're alive! Next patient, please!"

We roared so loud our teacher had to shut the classroom door or we'd distract the kindergartners, who mostly annoy us.

"Wow, Ms. Hill, you've got a class of live ones here," Tom joked on his way out. "Bet they keep you running."

But I didn't miss the small moment when he walked over to Max's desk before leaving. Max's writer's notebook got slipped right into Tom's hands. He stood there reading and flipping the pages. Every so often, he looked into Max's eyes. Each time he seemed a little sad until the final page, something Max was in the middle of writing. Then he laughed out loud. Don't you know I had to squirm my body up like a worm and check it out? All I could see was the title. It read: "Ode to Tom." Didn't I tell you it would work out?

Next there's Willie, the number one writer. We are close friends now, although we are keeping it a secret from the boys. Here's how I know. He walked right up to me last month and asked me to meet him in private by the window pole. My heart was thumping against my tie-dyed T-shirt, let me tell you.

"Destiny, *everything is cook and curry now*," he told me.

His smile was dazzling, like the one I first saw when his team won the soccer championship way back last June. That smile can fill a whole playground. It filled me up, too, so that I finally knew he wasn't speaking about food, or about cooking, or even about curry. I finally got it! He was telling me that this moment was perfect. And it was.

He showed me his grandma's letter. I saw my name written on it. I believe I blushed. Willie stared at me as if seeing me for the very first time. I got belly butterflies to feel his dark eyes searching through me.

I wonder what he sees in me.

You know, everyone has this impression of me like I'm extroverted and not sensitive and I'm way out there. Which I am. But I'm really getting to have deep thoughts, particularly as they're not flying out my mouth anymore. My ideas are getting trapped on the page instead.

Ms. Hill gave us a gift to remind us of just that. When we returned from lunch one day, each of us had our own copy of *KIDWRITERS of 5E* on our desk. A shiny book published at Staples, bound tight, with a copy of everyone's contest entries inside, the winners up front.

When you see the ideas that were once just floating in your head, all done up in bold black print, you can't believe it. Those ideas were once your feelings, your memories, some of them private, words you never said aloud. You don't even know how they happened to hop out of you. Here's the proof in black and white. Stories are surprises, their own magic.

I want to tie up all the loose ends of the year with ribbons and wrap it up like a present. This time I won't blab it. I'll write it down instead. But if you ask what we learned, some kids will know—the girls, mostly. Maybe even Max, but he won't say. Only Ms. Hill knew all along.

Who We Are
All we needed was a push
a little tap to point us in the right direction,
to get us started.
Just the right stories to float through our minds.

We aimed our pencil tips to the page.
When the words moved through us,
they made our little lives shine.
We never guessed.
We never knew.
We are the promises.
We are the poems.

JUNE

"Out of silence and listening,
a poem begins."
–Maximo

THE LAST WORD

Maximo

The final week of June, the sun beats down on
the tar roof, trapping a heat wave inside PS 1.
Willie says it's hot enough inside to jerk chicken.
Our T-shirts cling to our backs. My hair is
soaked just from thinking. After lunch Ms. Hill
lines us up. She says we radiate. We fill our
water bottles, grab our notebooks, and head to
the end of the hall. It's shady and quiet there
like sitting beneath a maple tree. We plop
down on the cool concrete floor to write. Gio

closes his eyes, dazed from the heat. Pencils scratch over the last pages of our notebooks.

Writing Time
We sit with our backs
against the cool wall.
Sneakers. Shorts. Bare legs.
Girls on one side.
Boys on the other.

Pencils scrape.
Thoughts darken
the pure white page
spreading shadows across it.
Voices call down the hallway.
Blue eyes look up.
Someone swats a fly away
then pencils aim at the page again.

Something is coming.
Out of silence
and listening
a poem begins.

Then, before the next pencil is sharpened, it's a half day, the very last day. The day we long waited for is here. Giovanni and I bounce down the steps smacking high fives. Wispy yellow streaks cover his head like some strange insect left tracks. His sister highlighted his hair for free with laundry bleach and Q-tips. That's not the worst of it. Most of it dripped on his poor little cousin Salvatore, who was once black-headed. Now the whole left side of his head is blond. All the kindergartners keep petting his hair like he's a zoo animal.

At the bottom of the steps, I stop. I have a strange feeling, like I didn't expect the ground to be there to hold me up. It's over way too fast. You know how you wait for some super event like your tenth birthday? You plan it so long, your brain lights up like Fourth of July fireworks just thinking about it. Then, in one night, it's over. History. It came and went too fast.

Beside me, Giovanni wastes no time. He's busy ripping his report card envelope apart.

"A two in reading! I won't be held over!" He jumps in the air. "Open yours!"

I do: 4s all the way down, even in writing! Best of all are Ms. Hill's final comments:

Maximo has made a wonderful adjustment this year. He's much improved in writing and in his spirits, too. I am proud of him and know that he will do well in sixth grade.

My whole chest swells up and I grin so hard, it hurts my face. I turn around to wave at Ms. Hill. She waves back, her wide skirt blowing in the June breeze like a celebration flag.

"Bye, Max!" Destiny screams as she runs past. "We're in the same class together next year. I promise not to bug you! You're my hero!!!"

Giovanni's right. Life happens in front of you. It could be a dust ball ready for a kick. Lin telling his first ever joke in English. Ramneet passing out of ESL. A copper curl dangling down Ashley's forehead. It's here right now. Today. Noon. This hot, hazy, humid New York day with the whole summer ahead, a stack of library books to read, and a new writer's notebook to fill. I'll even get postcards from Jamaica—Willie promised.

Maybe someday, there'll be a letter from my dad. Maybe not. For now, I'm living fine. Jones Beach and fresh, cool air is just a bus ride away. And guess who's going to learn how to make garlic balls with Gio's dad? Tiffany and Willie gave away their boxing tickets because they won't be in New York City this summer, so Gio and I are the lucky ones who'll be sitting beside Ms. Hill in Madison Square Garden watching Vinny the Hammer clobber his rival. HOOK 'EM, VINNY!

"See you in sixth grade!" I yell to all the fifth graders leaping in the air around me.

That's where I want to be. Up in the air, all summer long. Catching the sun. Living the stories. I won't come down until September.

GLOSSARIES

ITALIAN WORDS & PHRASES

addio	good-bye
brioche	Italian pastry
che cosa?	what?
chi?	who?
ciao	hello or good-bye
grazie	thank you
in vacanza	on holiday
mi sono smarrito	I'm lost
non capisco	I don't understand
per favore	please
quando?	when?
salute	cheers
scuzi	excuse me

JAMAICAN SLANG

all fruits ripe	all is good
bammy	bread
bashment	a happening or a party
batty an bench	inseparable
chatabax	chatterbox
chatty-chatty	talkative
chaka-chaka	messy
check it deep	check it out

chil'	child
crosses	troubles or problems
duppy	ghost
eased-up	relaxed
everything cook and curry	everything is just fine
fass	nosy
fit	ripe (such as fruit)
hightey-tightey	snobby
gaan	gone
irie	feeling great or happy
jerk	barbeque
labba-mout	big mouth
maga	skinny
main man	best friend
mon	everyone
move your backside	get up
obeah	spell
run a boat	a get-together
school boun fi gi recess	school is bound to have recess
sistren	women or girlfriends
su-su	gossip
walk good	good-bye, take care
wanga gut	hungry all the time
wa?/whaddup?	what?/what's up?

BIBLIOGRAPHY

CHILDREN'S BOOKS

Atwater, Florence, and Richard Atwater. *Mr. Popper's Penguins.* Boston: Little, Brown, 1938.

Brinckloe, Julie. *Fireflies.* New York: Macmillan, 1985.

Cooney, Barbara. *Miss Rumphius.* New York: Puffin/Viking Penguin, 1982.

Creech, Sharon. *Love That Dog.* New York: Harper Trophy/HarperCollins, 2001.

DiCamillo, Kate. *Because of Winn-Dixie.* Cambridge, Mass.: Candlewick Press, 2000.

Greenfield, Eloise, and Leslie Jones Little. *Childtimes.* New York: Thomas Y. Crowell, 1971.

Hest, Amy. *How to Get Famous in Brooklyn.* New York: Simon & Schuster, 1995.

Home. Edited by Michael J. Rosen. New York: Harper-Collins, 1992.

Lindgren, Astrid. *Pippi Longstocking.* New York: Puffin/Viking Penguin, 1997.

MacLachlan, Patricia. *Sarah, Plain and Tall.* New York: HarperTrophy/HarperCollins, 1985.

———. *What You Know First.* New York: Joanna Cotler Books/HarperCollins, 1995.

Paulsen, Gary. *Brian's Winter.* New York: Scholastic, 1996.

———. *Hatchet.* New York: Aladdin/Simon & Schuster, 1987.

————. *The River.* New York: Bantam Doubleday Dell, 1991.

————. *Woodsong.* New York: Scholastic, 1991.

Rylant, Cynthia. *Children of Christmas.* New York: Orchard Books, 1987.

————. *Every Living Thing.* New York: Simon & Schuster, 1988.

————. *Night in the Country.* New York: Bradbury Press, 1986.

————. *The Relatives Came.* New York: Bradbury Press, 1985.

————. *When I Was Young in the Mountains.* New York: E. P. Dutton/Viking Penguin, 1982.

Say, Allen. *Grandfather's Journey.* New York: Houghton Mifflin, 1993.

Silverstein, Shel. *Falling Up.* New York: Scholastic, 1996.

SUGGESTED READING

BOOKS ABOUT WRITING

Calkins, Lucy McCormick. *The Art of Teaching Reading*. New York: Addison-Wesley, 2001.

Goldberg, Natalie. *Writing Down the Bones*. Boston: Shambhala, 1986.

Graham, Paula W., ed. *Speaking of Journals*. Honesdale, Pa.: Boyds Mills Press, 1999.

King, Stephen. *On Writing*. New York: Pocket Books/ Simon & Schuster, 2000.

Muschla, Gary Robert. *The Writing Teacher's Book of Lists*. Englewood Cliffs, N.J.: Prentice Hall, 1991.

Tchudi, Susan, and Stephen Tchudi. *The Young Writer's Handbook*. New York: Macmillan, 1984.

Willis, Meredith Sue. *Blazing Pencils*. New York: Teachers and Writers Collaborative, 1990.

———. *Personal Fiction Writing*. New York: Teachers and Writers Collaborative, 1984.

Writers Express. A Handbook for Young Writers, Thinkers and Learners. Wilmington, Mass.: Write Source, D. C. Heath & Co., 1995.

AUTHOR'S NOTE

A tiny seed blew my way in the 1980s when, as a new teacher, I began my career in a crowded New York City classroom, empty of books. That seed was a Gould Grant offered through Columbia University, where I was studying "The Writing Process" taught by Lucy Calkins.

The grant awarded me with one thousand dollars worth of books. It brought to my bare classroom the rhythm, power, and magic of language with books like *When I Was Young in the Mountains, Night in the Country, Childtimes,* and *The Two of Them.* Memories flowed like rivers in response to them: a parent reminiscing about her one-room schoolhouse in Cyprus, a child telling of her flight from Afghanistan, a janitor singing childhood songs from South America. My room filled with family stories from all over the world. It reminded me of my own childhood when my family sat beneath a cherry tree on hot, summer nights listening to the stories our immigrant neighbors told.

The purpose of that grant was to study how the reading tastes of children are formed. The grant demanded tons of journals, logs, and notes about the children as they read and discussed what they were reading. I did form some theories about how children become lifelong readers. But the grant had hidden purposes. It brought unexpected gifts.

One of them was to transform a teacher into an observer. For once teachers notice something, they can direct their teaching to address it. For example, if students don't tell stories in sequence, that skill needs to be taught and reinforced in context. So I became a kidwatcher. I learned to expect the unexpected, as Donald Graves would say. The other gift was a surprise. I began to write daily. Whatever I observed, I jotted down quickly. Writer's notebooks and tiny memo pads that fit in my pocket filled up. Soon, it wasn't about reading anymore. I recorded descriptions of haircuts, lice checks, friendships, picture day, gym, and a child's response to divorce. Writing ignited my life. I became a writer along with my students. Writing was my passion.

"If only I could teach writing all day!" I joked with my principal.

In the 1990s, our school received Magnet funding from the federal government to develop our own program. Since we were already a Writing Process school, our staff wanted to deepen our commitment to writing. We became The Magnet School of Writing & Publishing. The publishing center, where we wrote and published our own books, became my new room. I was appointed staff developer, working with students from grades K–6 and their teachers. I taught the Writing Process as we wrote memoirs, personal narratives, poems, and nonfiction. We ended each year with a grand celebration in May, a week long Authors' and Artists' Fair. The gym overflowed with class books, individual books, vibrant artwork, and bright poetry posters mounted on chart stands.

This book spans those wonderful years I was teaching writing and observing my students. My characters are composites of children I have known, a bit of this boy, a part of this girl. Sometimes I picked up ideas just by observing; other times, I learned by listening to kids' stories, troubles, and wishes. Although I had over eighteen years of notetaking to draw upon when I decided to write a book about this experience, I couldn't quite figure out a way to present it.

Then one September, the catalyst arrived. Four fifth-grade classes with registers of thirty-six were stuffed into classrooms in the hottest part of the school. Although our parents and administration protested, another class never opened that year or the next. That was our biggest graduating class ever. It was also the year of lowest funding to maintain schools and no teacher contracts, yet vast monies spent on innovative reading, writing, and math programs rather than on reducing class size. My pencil began to move. I had my beginning.

Many programs and approaches to learning have come and gone since I became a teacher. Most last a few years and are forgotten. Some remain and are adopted by schools even after funding ends because they are practical and really work. As I write this, classes in my school still overflow. Every teacher knows the bitter truth—that learning is deeply affected when the student-to-teacher ratio is too high—because they have lived with it year in and out. This novel explores a little slice of utopia in a reduced class size. A classroom is a microcosm of society, a safe haven to learn how to find a place in the world. It's not about the next best program. It's all about creating a nurturing environment for kids. If teachers and students had the time and space to learn, we really would have that community of readers and writers I dreamed about as a new teacher in the 1980s.

V. F. S.